The Exeter Autl

is a group of professional writer
England. The EAA was set up in
from completely opposite sides of Devon, who managed to meet
occasionally in mid Devon as a central point. It was set up for the
simple reason all the other main writing groups were full.
Therefore I decided to set one up and create our own unique
stamp on literature events across England.

Over the years the EAA has expanded our membership to
professional writers from across Devon and Somerset.

The EAA runs two main literature events per year - Crime in the
Countryside (a festival of crime writing) and the Crediton
Literary Festival, celebrating all writing. These events are great
fun to organise and are real celebrations of the depth of writing
in the south-west.

Our members consist of both fiction and non-fiction authors,
playwrights, and poets. We give talks, lectures, and workshops
on our specialisms which include Devon folklore, history,
archaeology, space travel, Robin Hood, nursing, the psychology
of villains, and many, many more! So if you have a chance to
listen to their talks go and be entertained and probably a little
surprised!

P. J. Reed

Devon Air Ambulance

Devon Air Ambulance (DAA) is the Charity that raises the funds to keep two emergency Air Ambulances flying, to relieve injury and illness in the county of Devon. In 2018 it cost £7.5 million to run the service.

We are proud to be independent of Government and National Lottery Funding: this safeguards the service for the long-term and ensures we can deliver what the people of Devon tell us they want from their Air Ambulance.

DAA operates seven days a week and in 2019 we extended the service to operate until 2am. We are able to get to most of Devon within 10 minutes and the whole of Devon within 15, which ensures patients receive treatment within the critical period immediately following acute illness or an accident and are conveyed to the specialist treatment centre most appropriate for their needs, ensuring they receive the best possible care and giving them the best chance of survival.

In addition, DAA has substantially improved patient care through the creation of a ground-breaking Master's Degree for air paramedics aimed at making them amongst the highest qualified in the profession.

Devon's Air Ambulances are an essential part of the community we live in and the service would not be possible without the generous support and donations from the people, businesses and communities in and around Devon, every penny raised is making a real difference.

Tales

of

Deepest

Darkest

Devon

from the

Exeter Authors Association

Contents

The Dartmoor Dragon
By Jenifer Braund

Drusilla the dragon was very excited. Earlier she had woken up from a long sleep thinking she was the only dragon left in the whole world. She had felt very sad and lonely. As she had stretched and struggled to her feet, she had looked around and couldn't see a single thing she recognised. She had gone to sleep in a huge green forest, deep in a dark warm cave with her brothers and sisters. She remembered her father had gone off to help a volcano get its fire going. Her mother had gone to visit a distant wizard to renew her magic powers. She had sprinkled her last stardust over the little dragons to help them have magical dreams and keep them safe.

Drusilla must have slept the longest of them all, for the others were gone. So were the green forest and their cosy cave. She woke up among some huge grey granite rocks on a high windswept moor. She gave a terrible fright to a large black raven that had chosen Drusilla's grey back as a perch to have an after-dinner nap. You see, when a dragon sleeps it looks just like a big grey rock. Unless you know dragons very well, it's hard to tell a dragon and a rock apart. They breathe so slowly you can't even see a movement and they sleep very soundly.

So why was Drusilla so excited? You may well ask. When Raven recovered from his fright, he felt just a bit sorry for Drusilla. It must be terrible, he thought, to wake up and find yourself all alone. He told her she was on Dartmoor in a corner of England called Devonshire. He had set out to find if any of the other Dartmoor ravens knew of the whereabouts of any other dragons.

He flew all afternoon from one end of the great moor to the other. He spoke to seven wise ravens. These were the ravens that guarded the moor; one to the east, one to the west, one to the north and one to the south. The fifth raven watched over the moor from above, the sixth from the underworld and the seventh, the oldest and wisest of all, guarded the Invisible World. He was the keeper of the magic. Raven approached each in turn with the same question.

'Please have you seen any dragons lately?' The first four each looked at him with great amusement.

'Hello, young raven, where have you come from? There haven't been any dragons for thousands of years, everyone knows that.'

Young Raven protested, 'But there are, I know there are, I've met one. I was sitting on her when she woke up.'

They laughed kindly and one said, 'Well, youngster, what a wonderful dream you had. I like to dream of dragons; they are magical creatures from long ago.' The North Raven chuckled, 'They had such a fearsome reputation, people became afraid of them, but really they were gentle, helpful creatures. If someone needed to light a fire or clear a clearing for planting, there would always be a friendly dragon around, ready to breathe fire and help out. Useful things dragons, a bit soft, people used to take advantage of them, having them run around lighting this and burning that. No wonder the poor creatures became extinct, they were worn out with all that fire-raising.'

This was getting interesting; the only dragon Young Raven had ever heard of was the one in the story killed by St George for terrorising the townspeople. But the four could tell him no more. Try Sky Raven, they told him, he's older than us and remembers the old days better than we do.

Now there is a strange thing about ravens. Though they often seem solitary birds, they all seem to be connected in some way. They can communicate with each other just by thinking, so that by the time Young Raven reached the Sky Raven it was very clear that he was expected. Sky Raven didn't laugh when Young Raven asked about dragons. He actually asked about Drusilla and even agreed to return with him to talk to her. Drusilla felt much better when Young Raven, her only friend, returned with such a wise and friendly companion.

~ ~ ~ ~

It was from the Sky Raven that Drusilla learned about the changes in the land. How over thousands of years, the climate had changed from being very hot and wet, with forests covering all of England. The few scattered peoples that lived in the forest grew in numbers and people from different lands came to explore, fight and conquer. They took slaves to a distant land called Rome and they searched for and captured baby dragons because they were so useful as fire-lighters, as well as being gentle and willing companions. As more people came, trees were cut down and crops were planted in fields. Over the centuries, the landscape changed. High ground became windswept moor and the trees, caves and forests where dragons liked to live gradually disappeared.

'So,' said the Sky Raven, 'your brothers and sisters may have been taken all over the world.'

'But what about my father?' said Drusilla. 'He went to help a volcano find its fire.'

'To find that out, we will have to ask Sixth Raven, who guards the underworld.'

Luckily for Drusilla, the entrance to the underworld was situated in the heart of the moor. With her two companions leading the way, Drusilla followed. While they flew and hopped, she ambled along slowly, getting the feel of her legs, which were feeling rather stiff after a sleep lasting thousands of years.

~ ~ ~ ~

It was some hours later when Sky Raven suddenly flew ahead almost out of sight. Young Raven kindly stayed with Drusilla as she ambled along, enjoying the countryside, which yielded distant views of something silvery and sparkling many miles away. Drusilla couldn't quite make it out and was about to ask when Sky Raven returned with a very old raven indeed. Larger than any they had met so far, the raven of the underworld was so black and shiny that his feathers sparkled in the sunshine. Drusilla could just see her reflection and was rather surprised to see she was quite a lot larger than she remembered. Then Drusilla got another surprise for, inside her head, she heard the words, 'Don't worry, Dragon, in thousands of years you are bound to have grown, you know. You were only a baby when you fell asleep, now you are almost grown up.'

'Almost?' thought Drusilla, well how old do dragons get? Almost before the thought was thought, came a thought reply.

'They live for ever.'

Drusilla found herself looking around to see whom she was having this strange inside-her-head conversation with. All she could see were the three black birds: her friend Young Raven, Sky Raven their guide and this very old, very black raven Sky Raven introduced as the Guardian of the underworld. Drusilla couldn't see a smile, how can a bird with a beak for a mouth smile? But she could somehow feel the smile, and there was a sort of knowing inside, that here was a wise friend. Sky Raven hopped onto Drusilla's shoulder and spoke in her ear. 'Young Raven and I can only speak outwardly, though we can communicate with our own species and with each other, in our heads. The wise one, though, has lived so long he has never lost the ancient gifts. It's him you can hear inside your head and he can hear you. In the old time, everyone could talk inside their heads. But since they invented language and writing and books, everyone gradually lost the gift. Bit of a knack to it, you see, you have to be tuned into it, on the right wave-length.' He cocked his head on one side so he was almost eye to eye with Drusilla, checking out that she understood. Drusilla was struggling to understand. It was a slow process. When she had fallen asleep under the protection of the stardust, she was such a baby her communication system was only just developing. Her parents seemed to know what she wanted without talking inside or outside. When she wasn't sleeping, she played with her brothers and sisters.

'I don't think I could even breathe smoke, let alone make fire.'

No sooner had she had the thought she took a long, slow, deep breath and huffed.

'Wow,' she nearly jumped out of her skin. Young Raven, who had been sitting on a rock a few feet in front, took off vertically like a rocket. Just in time, for the rock he had been sitting on was enveloped in fire from Drusilla's huff. First it glowed red, then deep orange, then silvery gold, then white hot. It was so hot Drusilla had to move away and Sky Raven clung on tight to her shoulders, as waves of heat rolled over them both. The Guardian gave a great raven croak, soared over the white-hot rock and flew higher and higher on the waves of heat he called thermals until he was a tiny black speck high in the sky above the moor.

Then something wonderful happened. Inside her head, Drusilla had a picture of the moor, the hills and valleys from very high in the sky. She looked and looked, the higher the old raven went, the further she could see. The Guardian was sending his view of the world into her head. She could see forever. Then something even stranger happened. Not only could she see from high up she seemed to be able to see back over the years.

~ ~ ~ ~

The landscape below started to change, as if a movie film was being run backwards. The bare moor with its great granite outcrops became softer, covered with grass and shrubs. There were fields bound with stone walls. Now and then there were village communities; once a huge fire swept across the moor so that it was blackened and burned. Trees lost their leaves and were left charred. Just after the fire or was it before, a huge storm shook the land, lightning lit up the moor and thunder crashed. Drusilla could see the storm and the fire, she could even hear the thunder and smell the burning and feel the heat. But all without fear as she knew in some strange way of knowing, that the Guardian was sharing his memories from long ago. Because Drusilla was born two thousand years ago, she could receive the memories, the sights and smells and sounds through which she had slept.

Still the landscape changed as hundreds of years sped past, lighting up pictures in her head. She was so absorbed she almost missed what the show was all about. For as the past came nearer, so the moor became thick and heavy with forest. Bare rocks could no longer be seen, undergrowth hid them from sight and large forest trees grew up all around.

Then Drusilla became aware of the Guardian circling wider and wider, so the field of view changed. A great hill, topped with thick forest, came into view. The Guardian flew down closer to the ground and seemed to be searching for something. What was he looking for? Then Drusilla saw something she recognised. Deep in the forest a beautiful sparkling river wound in a deep ravine, the trees reaching to its edges. Something about it stirred an old memory, so that her heart leapt. That something felt like 'home'. The Guardian sensed Drusilla's recognition and spiralled down and down and down until he was hovering over the forest. Closer now, Drusilla could see a deep rushing river, sparkling and crashing down over a rocky riverbed.

'Lower,' she urged, 'lower.' The Guardian swooped down until he was moving in slow and lazy flight a few feet above the sparkling river. Drops of water bounced off the rocks, covering him with glistening spray. As he felt it, so did Drusilla and she chuckled to feel drops of clear icy water over her dry leathery skin. She was nearly home.

~ ~ ~ ~

'There,' she urged, 'over there, round the next bend, up over that overhang. There, there are the caves, there is my home.' There indeed was home and Drusilla was there, and this was a mystery. For the Drusilla that she was now wasn't the same Drusilla who was sitting in the entrance to the cave. The Drusilla she saw was a baby dragon who was looking very alertly at a large black raven that alighted on a rock just by the entrance of the cave. Drusilla had the very strange experience of looking into her own eyes. The baby dragon was looking right into her eyes because it was looking into the eyes of the big shiny black raven.

Drusilla was startled and confused. The picture remained, with the baby dragon at its centre. A kindly voice in her head said,

'This is 'paradox'.' Before she could ask Guardian said, 'A paradox is something that cannot be but is. You know it cannot possibly be yet you are seeing it, so it must be. Don't worry about it,' the Guardian said, 'it's a touch of magic. It's the kind of thing that makes all things possible if only you really believe. When you were a baby dragon, your parents protected you with magic. It was such a powerful magic that it kept you asleep for two thousand years, kept you hidden in the shape of a rock deep in the forest, so that no one could ever harm you. That is why you still have the ability to understand magic, to communicate in the old ways and when you meet another creature, who knows the old ways, you see what they see, hear what they hear and smell and feel; now that is magic.'

It was a lot to take in. It made Drusilla's brain ache. She apologised to the Guardian, she couldn't think any more for now, so could she just look, please? Somehow she felt the raven withdraw from inside her mind though she could still see him. As she looked, her brothers and sisters came out of the cave. One by one, she counted them until there were seven baby dragons playing at the cave mouth. Baby Drusilla was almost the smallest, with one exception. A very little dragon came up and rested his snout across her tail. He too was looking at the raven and, it seemed, straight into Drusilla's eyes. This was Trevor, her youngest brother.

The remembering of his name brought back the memory of the others. She looked and saw Dirk and Hamish and Dylan and Erik and then, she spotted her sister Dulcima, who was swinging on their mother's great horny tail. She was so happy to see her mother and her brothers and sister. But no matter how hard she looked she couldn't see her father.

She felt Guardian's comforting silence. 'I think we are looking at your family just after your father left to go and help the volcano. To find him, we need to return to the present, and then we can go and talk to Seventh Raven, who has even greater magic. Seventh Raven guards the gateway to the Invisible World.

He can show you what no one else can see, human or creature or dragon. He can see into the spiritual world, which, unless you trust in him and believe in the invisible and the impossible, you cannot see. Drusilla, do you believe in the invisible? Can the impossible happen? Do you want to see your father badly enough to trust the Seventh Raven?'

Drusilla desperately wanted to make sure her father was safe and well. She wasn't sure if she did believe in an invisible world but she did believe in magic. For hadn't her mother dusted her with magic stardust to protect her? Drusilla was a very truthful dragon. 'I want to believe,' she said silently. 'I want very much to believe. Is that enough?'

'We'll go and see if it is. We will ask the Seventh Raven.'

~ ~ ~ ~

As if a spell had broken Drusilla was no longer looking at the cave but at the bare windswept moor, with the Guardian soaring overhead. On one shoulder, she felt comforted to have Sky Raven. Glancing over her shoulder, she could see her friend Young Raven balancing precariously on the very tip of her very long tail. She swished it slightly, making it swing. He fluttered his wings to balance himself. Guardian perched on the rock that had now cooled down after Drusilla's practice fire breathing.

'To reach the Seventh Raven,' he said, 'we have to enter the Inner Realms, so I want you to do exactly as I say.'

Drusilla questioned silently, 'Can we all go together, can my friends come?'

'As long as they choose freely, they can accompany you.'

The Seventh Raven looked at Sky Raven and Young Raven, both were ready for the adventure. Since Young Raven had found Drusilla, he had no intention of letting 'his friend' out of his sight. The three friends looked at the Guardian and listened carefully.

'Breathe deeply,' that was easy enough, 'now empty your mind and let go.'

Young Raven wasn't quite sure what that meant. He felt sure that, if he let go of his firm hold on Drusilla's tail, he might fall off. However, he did his best.

All three became aware of the voice of the Guardian, like tinkling music inside their heads,

'I want you to imagine you are on a path in the middle of a beautiful forest. Sunlight is streaming through the trees. You can hear birds singing a little way off. Walk deeper into the forest and let go of all your thoughts. Silence your inner chatter.' That was very hard for Young Raven. 'Only think of the forest path, feel the soft green moss and crunchy leaves beneath your feet. Reach out and touch the rough bark of the trees. Smell the scent of wild flowers, pick a leaf of wild sorrel and taste it in your mouth.' Raven liked that bit a lot. 'Now follow the sound of water deeper and deeper into the forest.'

The three friends looked as though they were asleep. Yet none of them was, for inside their minds in their imagination they were walking together down a beautiful forest path. Now they could all hear the water. Sky Raven flew slightly ahead, leading the way. Drusilla felt a flutter of excitement. When they came to the water the path wound alongside the stream for a little way. Then the stream and the path plunged downhill, a beautiful waterfall, splashing down a steep drop, until it disappeared into the green hillside below. The friends clambered down carefully, their wings making it easier for the ravens. Drusilla clung on with her horny claws her leathery wings helping her to balance. When they reached the place where the stream disappeared, the path followed. Deep into the hillside it dipped, gently at first, gradually getting steeper as it went into the heart of the mountain. Where it was steepest, there were steps like a staircase.

Drusilla noticed the walls were getting smoother. The Guardian's voice became softer,

'Now find yourself going down into a shimmering cave, the steps before you shining and silvery leading you into a beautiful crystal cavern. Walk into the cavern and look for the Seventh Raven.'

Drusilla spotted him first though she wasn't quite sure if it was he, for he wasn't black, he sort of sparkled before changing into a beautiful bird shape. It was as if he wasn't really a bird but more like the idea of a bird. The strangest feeling came from him, a presence of something very special, something invisible but something we all know and recognise. Drusilla felt surrounded by love, it made her feel very safe. She drew close and spoke shyly.

'Is my father with you? Have you seen him? Can you take me to him?'

The light sparkled and swelled, filling up the cavern and surrounding the three friends. The Seventh Raven spoke like Sky Raven, a gentle silvery 'voice' inside their heads. Another journey was about to start a journey to the heart of the volcano to see Drusilla's father.

~ ~ ~ ~

They sensed rather than felt movement, for as they were standing the crystal cavern seemed to move past them. The walls changed from crystal to silver to gold and back to crystal again. Drusilla was certain the walls were speeding by them yet they seemed not to move. Sky Raven stayed close at one shoulder and at some time on the journey Young Raven had arrived on her other shoulder. Guardian seemed not to be with them, though the Seventh Raven was all about them, as if they were somehow within it, or even nestling between its great translucent wings. Drusilla couldn't make sense of it. After all, how can a two thousand year-old dragon ride on the wings of a raven that you couldn't even see, let alone feel? Drusilla decided it must be a bit like riding a cloud. Something kept you up there, safe and secure, but it wasn't something you could make sense of with your common sense. Rather, you had to use your sense of magic and trust and believe in something special.

As Drusilla was thinking about these things, she noticed something else. The walls of their underground passageway had changed to black-grey rock but the deeper they went the more the rock glowed.

Being a fire dragon, she sensed heat. The walls were becoming hotter and hotter until they glowed red. They were getting closer to the heart of the mountain, and the living volcano at its core. Drusilla didn't mind the heat one little bit but she was a bit worried about her friends. Of course the Seventh Raven had everything under control. As she was revelling in the heat, the ravens were looking cool and unflustered. Round each was a glowing, sparkling circle of cool air, more magic! The voice spoke inside Drusilla's head.

'We are near your father now. Though you may not recognise his outward appearance you will know it is he.' Drusilla wasn't sure what the Seventh Raven meant. Before she could ask the passage opened out into a vast cavern, so huge the friends couldn't see the other side but they could see the bottom, or what looked like the bottom. They were looking down on an ocean of heaving molten lava. They had reached the very core of the volcano and were looking down on a magma lake. It was so hot that the rock in the middle of the mountain had melted into liquid living flame. Rivers of molten lava flowed from distant places into the lake.

Here, though she couldn't see him, Drusilla knew she had found her father. He had given up his dragon nature to become the living fire that gave the volcano life. As she sensed his presence, she knew he sensed hers, for she was filled with such a tremendous feeling of being loved. She felt a part of him for a while and they talked though not with words. He told her about his journey and why he was the only creature who could save the volcano. Drusilla's heart swelled up with love and pride. Then answering her unspoken question he talked of another journey she would have to undertake if she was to find her mother. At last it was time to say goodbye.

Drusilla's sadness at leaving so soon was swiftly replaced by a tremor of excitement. Her father's voice became the roar of a huge underground explosion echoing around the vast cavern. Yet they were not outside listening, they were inside the sound. It was reverberating inside out and outside in. They were filled with it and part of it. They were about to take the most exciting ride of their lives, the volcano was ready to erupt. It did so every three hundred and thirty-three years. They had arrived at just the right time. The Seventh Raven still enclosed them with its magical silvery light. Within it they settled just above the boiling rock, just like waiting for a rocket to take off.

~ ~ ~ ~

Before they could take another breath, there was a great rushing sound and they rode the sea of lava as it exploded through the top of the mountain. They went up and up and up so fast it took their breath almost right away, which is a hard thing to do with dragons because they have so much breath. It felt a bit like going up in a very fast elevator; up to the thousandth floor. Except they weren't enclosed in a box but in a silvery bubble whose walls you could see through. The colours of the molten rock, scarlet and red, orange and brownish yellow, all constantly mingling and changing, a beautiful upward gushing river, all the hot colours of the rainbow, so close you could put your hand out and touch them. Drusilla reached out to touch, but their transport accommodated her wing, flowing itself around her outstretched claw. It was protecting them yet somehow allowing them to protrude into the boiling magma as it carried them among the rocks and debris up through the centre of the Earth.

With a final bone-shaking crash, the top of the mountain exploded upwards and outwards, showering hundreds of tons of rubble high into the sky. The silver light bubble flew with it, soaring higher and higher into the sky on a great fountain of fiery ashes and lava.

Drusilla felt rather than heard her father saying goodbye. She also felt his sense of satisfaction from a job well done. The volcano was happy it had fulfilled its promises by erupting on time. The forest and the countryside were happy because the landscape would be enriched with iron and minerals from the centre of the Earth. The forest would again grow thick and strong as the lava cooled down. And all the animals and birds, who had known with that bit of them inside that knows these things, to move away while the volcano played, would move back. New caves, new rock formations and, most important of all, new magic places for those who knew where to find them. That was Drusilla's father's contribution, though his gift to Drusilla and the ravens wasn't yet finished. He had known that Drusilla desperately wanted to find her mother. Special people know these things, those people with the touch of magic.

In helping the volcano and giving Drusilla that fiery ride from the centre of the Earth through the mountain and high into the sky, her father had given her a very special gift. With the help of Seventh Raven and the silver light travelling machine, he had projected them all on their way to the stars. That is why Drusilla was so excited at the beginning of our story. For when

Young Raven returned with Sky Raven and all these adventures started, Young Raven knew they were actually on their way to the stars. For that is where the wizard lived whom Drusilla's mother had visited two thousand years ago. They were about to travel on another amazing adventure – but that's another story.

Are We There Yet?
By Richard Dee

I couldn't help asking, I had just woken up, the car slowing down had jolted me out of a dream, it was dark outside but there was a faint glow in the sky, morning was coming.

'No,' my mother said calmly, 'not yet.'

Argentia, my sister, punched me on the shoulder, 'you always say that,' she mocked. 'at least you waited till we were out of the drive this time.'

I leaned over, as far as my seat belt would let me and swung my hand at her. She dodged; my intended slap missed. Her head banged against the side window. 'Ouch,' she screamed, 'Dad, help, the brat's attacking me again.'

My father sighed, 'pack it in, you're both as bad as each other. You two need to learn how to get along.'

'Why couldn't you have dropped me off yesterday?' asked Argentia, ignoring him. Now it was Mother's turn to sigh.

'I'm sorry darling,' she said, 'Felicity's parents asked me to bring you over this morning, and it's on the way.'

At least she would be gone soon, and I'd have my best friend with me for the next two weeks. Argentia was off to France, she's been invited to stay with Felicity Hughes-Morrison from school; my reward was to bring a friend to the caravan in Devon. It meant that we could put the getting along thing off for a while longer.

I had never been abroad, Argentia had been everywhere. Sibling jealousy wasn't really a suitable way of looking at it. Argentia's life had been so much better. Older by five years, she had benefitted from my father's job, she had the ballet lessons, riding lessons and the posh school. I had started at the school too; and been farmed out for the holidays, while my mum and dad worked abroad, she swanned off on foreign trips with her friends.

'Your turn will come,' said Mum, 'when you're a little older,' as I'd watched her head to somewhere exciting. I'd been left to cry myself to sleep. And get told how wonderful it had all been when she got home.

Then; my dad had lost his job, just when I should have been starting to benefit. No pony for me, or ballet. Not that I could have managed it; as all my teachers were so keen to tell me, I had at least two left feet. With the loss of Dad's income, we had been removed from the boarding school and sent to a place run by a posse of what seemed to me like sadistic nuns.

It meant that, as well as all term, we got to be together in the holidays as well! Now that Dad wasn't working abroad; holidays were trips to the seaside, or the once a year visit to Torbay, where we rented a caravan.

Except that this year, Tia had got on so well with new girl Felicity that she was invited to keep her company. I was on my own again. Then I had the brainwave, Maisie was my best friend at school, I asked if she could come with me. To my surprise, everyone said yes.

Which was a result, once we had dumped Tia, we could pick her up and head to the coast. It would be a lot more fun in Devon with someone my own age.

'I don't want to spend the holiday with you anyway,' Tia said, as she got out of the car at Felicity's house. 'You only want to do boring things, nothing exciting will happen.'

'Don't care,' I answered. 'I'd rather be bored with Maisie than bored with you anyway; except I won't be, cos she's fun and you aren't.'

'Goodbye dear, be good and we'll see you soon,' said Mum, watching Dad struggle to lift her suitcase out of the car, what was she taking with her? Who knew, she was gone before she could be bothered to say goodbye.

Next stop was Maisie's house, she was wide awake and full of plans. 'I've never been to Devon,' she said, after we had hugged. 'I've never stayed in a caravan either, it'll be such a laugh. Thanks for inviting me, Mrs Pett.'

You're very welcome dear,' she said, 'Andorra talks about you all the time.'

She shot me a look, she needn't have worried, I wouldn't have told her any of it, but I think the nuns might have spilt the beans. Not content with spoiling my time at school with silly ideas about learning and not laughing, they seemed determined to spoil my home life as well. Mainly by getting Dad upset, why else would they keep writing to him about me?

We giggled and talked all the way down the road, as the sun climbed in the cloudless sky. Mum passed us sandwiches and drinks for breakfast.

'It won't be long now,' Dad told us as we passed Newton Abbot, the main roads soon gave way to tiny lanes as we drove deeper into the countryside. Of course, we found a car to get stuck behind, moving at about three miles an hour in the narrowest parts. It was old and streaked with what looked like seagull poo, the back windows all covered with thick curtains.

Foreigners!' said Dad, as it suddenly stopped and he had to stand on the brakes again. A huge tractor squeezed past us, smelling of cows.

'How do you know that?' I asked.

'The driver's on the other side of the car,' he said.

'They drive on the wrong side of the road abroad,' added Mum.

I'd never been, it sounded dangerous, although I suppose if they all did it, it might be OK. Funny how Tia had never mentioned it.

'Look at the number plate,' he added, 'that's another clue.' I looked and it was so different from ours. Instead of an orange oblong with black letters, this one was white; the letters were blue and in a strange order. I looked again, saw an association between them. I started to laugh, Maisie joined in, even though she might not have noticed what I'd seen she always did that, we set each other off all the time. Hence why we were kept so far apart at school.

'What are you laughing at?' asked Mum, when it had gone on for several minutes.

'It's the letters,' I gasped, 'in the number plate. They make a word.'

Mum; bless her was still oblivious, 'one, three, U, M?' she said, 'I don't..., Oh.'

'BUM,' shrieked Maisie, then she collapsed into more giggles.

I could see Dad's neck going red, 'we don't say that Maisie,' he muttered.

'Andorra does,' she replied, 'at school, all the time.' Thanks very much, ex-friend.

Dad sighed, 'I know, the teachers write and tell me.' He thought for a moment, 'perhaps, if you say thirteen, it might keep you out of trouble, you both would know what you meant, you could explain it to everyone else and the teachers wouldn't be able to stop you saying it.'

'Thirteen, um,' I experimented. This time everyone laughed. Meanwhile, the foreign car was still in front, still moving one wheel at a time. I wanted to get to the caravan, I recognised the road, we were only a mile or so away.

'It'll be gone in a while,' Mum said optimistically, but it wasn't and when we got to our campsite, it turned in ahead of us. But it didn't stop by the reception area, it kept going, bumping down the road towards the trees that fringed our field, with its rows of neatly spaced caravans. Each one was raised up on a ramp over the lane, once we had our keys and van number, Dad had to drive the car up the slope to park clear of the lane, so that everyone else could get past us.

'I wonder who that was?' Maisie said; as we watched it disappear into the other field, the one meant for tents. 'Goodness knows,' said Dad, 'it didn't look very nice, keep well away from it you two.'

'Perhaps it's a murderer,' I whispered, trying to make my voice sound all evil. Maisie looked worried. 'Don't,' she said, 'I'll never sleep.'

As if that was going to happen. Maisie could sleep anywhere, lessons, lunchtime, whenever. At least she didn't snore, much. We unloaded the car; we were sharing a small bedroom with two narrow bunks while Mum and Dad had the other one. There was a tiny bathroom with a shower, a kitchen as part of the lounge and that was it.

'Do you want a cup of tea?' asked Mum. 'No thanks,' I answered, 'I'm going to show Maisie around.' Leaving her telling us to be careful, we ran across the grass towards a set of swings and a slide, it was where any children on the site met up and hung out. Through a fold in the hills, I could see the sea, it might have only been a blue line but seeing it reminded me that I would be paddling in it very soon.

The swings were deserted except for Jake, his parents owned the site and I remembered him from last year. He was a little bit older than me; Tia had pronounced him 'fit' and had delighted in embarrassing him, making him go red and stutter, which I

27

thought was unfair because he was really quite nice. Jake was wearing shorts and a tee shirt, his arms burnt brown by the sun. 'Hey Andi,' he said when he saw me, 'you're back again, where's your stuck-up sister?' So that was what he thought of her, I could use that when I got home; when she was being annoying.

Maisie laughed, 'that sounds like Tia,' she said. I agreed, Tia was so aloof, she acted her age in dog years. Especially around anyone younger and less posh than she thought she was, 'she's gone to France with her friend,' I told him. 'This is Maisie.'

'Hi Maisie,' he said. 'Great to see you; welcome to sunny Devon.' She smiled.

'Jake, we saw a foreign car, all dirty, it came in in front of us and went into the field where the tents go. Do you know anything about it?'

He looked upset and worried, I'd never seen that from him before, he was pretty fearless and knew all about the countryside, he'd shown me bird's nests in the woods and all sorts of interesting things. 'That must be the one my dad was on about, a late booking, he arrived two days ago. He's a bird watcher or something, he wanted peace and quiet so we said he could park his van up in the woods. He must have been out getting food. The caravan matches the car, it's old and dirty.'

'Let's go and have a look,' I suggested. Jake shook his head, 'I wouldn't. I haven't been up to the woods since he got here, only once. The man's not friendly, he goes out at night and sleeps in the day. I went up there, just looking around, not being nosey or anything. I mean; I live here. He shouted at me, told me to stay away or he'd tell my dad I was bothering him.'

'Never mind his dirty old caravan,' Maisie said, 'it's not why we're here.'

Before we could say anything else, Mum called us for lunch. 'We're going into Paignton,' she said, 'you can go to the beach.'

'Come on Maisie, let's have a bag of chips and a paddle,' I suggested.

'Donuts on the Pier,' added Maisie.

'Lucky old you,' said Jake, 'I could do with going to the beach, I hardly ever get there. I've got to help my dad this afternoon. See you later.'

'What does Jake mean?' said Maisie as we walked back to our home on wheels. 'He lives by the sea; he must go there a lot.'

'He told me before,' I explained, 'because he can go anytime, he hardly ever does, he says everyone who lives here's the same.'

'Strange,' she answered, 'I'd be there every day.'

We all got into the car and Dad reversed down the ramp into the lane. 'What do you want to do first?' asked Mum.

~ ~ ~ ~

We spent a great afternoon, but I couldn't get the caravan out of my head, or that the man had been rude to Jake. How dare he, Jake was my friend, he lived here, even if you were paying, there was no need to be rude. I had a plan; we could play a trick on him.

I told Maisie my idea when I got her alone on the beach. 'I don't like that man upsetting Jake, we need to do something to his car, or his caravan, just to mess him up, teach him a lesson.'

'What can we do?' she wondered, 'I don't know anything about cars, or caravans.' Neither did I but I knew someone who did.

'Remember Millie Tipping, before she got expelled? She had a great array of practical jokes to play on the teachers.'

'Oh yeah, her,' Maisie said.

'I remember once, she rammed mud into the headmaster's cars exhaust pipe so the engine wouldn't start.' She told me that she got the idea from her brother, at that special school he went to.'

'What was special about it?' she asked. 'I thought it was a rough school, full of troublemakers.'

'It can't have been rough, she said it was approved by the council.'

She gave me a strange look, perhaps it meant something else. We could sort it out later, the point was I knew some pranks we could play on Mr Foreign Car for upsetting Jake. I was prepared to bet that Tia wasn't as full of useful information as Millie Tipping had been.

'Oh yeah, that was fun, he got ever so upset.' Maisie was grinning, 'and there was the time that she put nail varnish into the keyholes of all the lockers in the staffroom.'

'I've got some nail varnish in my things. That ought to do it.'

'When?'

'After tea, we'll say we're going to meet Jake and his friends.'

It was still a beautiful day, when we had eaten, we put the plan into operation.

~ ~ ~ ~

We crept around the caravan, which was as dirty and clapped out as the car that had pulled it here.

'Thirteen,' said Maisie and I couldn't help it, I started to laugh. 'Shh,' she said. I shut up as I realised that I might be heard by anyone inside.

All the curtains were drawn, nothing moved. We stood still for a moment, ready to run.

'He must be asleep,' I whispered. There was no answer, I turned around. Maisie had vanished. I started to panic, looked back at the van.

There was a tall, thin man standing in front of me, pale skin and long greasy hair. Where had he come from? The caravan door was still closed. He had a stained tee shirt and jeans, no shoes.

'What do you want?' he asked, his voice rough, his hands raised. I stepped back and fell over, he loomed over me as I scrabbled backwards through the grass and branches, trying to get away from him.

'Well?' he demanded.

There was a sound like someone stepping on a twig. He turned towards it, Maisie appeared around the side of the caravan, she had a stick in her hands, nearly as big as she was. 'Get away from her,' she said.

As I got to my feet, he backed away. I saw movement in the curtains at one of the windows. 'Clear off,' the man said, 'and don't come back.'

We ran.

'Did you see that?' I asked Maisie; when we were back in the other field. Fortunately, he wasn't following us.

'What?'

'The curtains, they moved, someone else was in there with him.'

'I didn't see it; I was trying to hold the stick and watch him. Perhaps it's his girlfriend.'

'Urgh, Maisie, that's disgusting. He was filthy and smelly.'

'Let's not tell anyone and keep out of the way.' It sounded like a good idea. He would be bound to blame us, being a grownup Dad would agree with him and we would be in trouble. It was so unfair.

'That was very brave,' I realised that I was shaking, tears came into my eyes. I brushed them away. 'You coming to my rescue like that.'

She shrugged, 'it's what we do, we're friends. You can rescue me one day.'

'Of course I will,' I said.

We kept quiet when we got back to the caravan, Mum and Dad were engrossed in something on the T.V. so we showered and got into bed without having to explain why my jeans were muddy and I'd been crying.

Next morning, I was awoken by the sound of seagulls walking on the roof of the caravan. At least, I thought it was, when they got louder, I realised that it was raining, hard.

'We'll have to stay here today,' said Dad, 'I'll drive into town and get some stuff to keep you amused.'

He came back with newspapers, magazines and some sweets for us.

It was a boring day, we read, watched daytime T.V. and played cards, but the next morning, the sun shone brightly again.

We spent a few days exploring, we went to the beach again, several times, and up onto Dartmoor, where we picnicked by a river and splashed in the cold, clear water. We went to the zoo and had a trip on a steam train. And we had lots of ice-cream.

We had almost forgotten about the strange man, then we went shopping in Paignton.

We were in the chemist's, Dad had sunburn; Mum had told him to be careful, but he hadn't listened. The atmosphere was frosty, he went into a different shop to us. We were queueing up when Maisie nudged me. 'He's in front of us,' she whispered, 'the man from the caravan. What should we do?'

'What can we do, let's keep quiet and hope he doesn't spot us,' I said.

We could see what he was buying, children's cough medicine and herbal sleeping tablets that I recognised, Mum used them sometimes. He seemed preoccupied and never noticed us.

We saw him again, as we wandered around all the shops selling things for the beach and funny souvenirs that my dad called 'tat'. This time, he bought some small tee shirts, ones that would never fit him, with unicorns and mermaids on them.

'He must have got a child up in that caravan with him,' Maisie said as we watched.

'They're girls' shirts. I told you I saw something in the window.'

'Why hasn't she come out with him, if she's only got a cough? He shouldn't have left her in there on her own.'

'Perhaps she can't move?'

'Then he should get someone to stay with her,' Maisie was indignant, 'make sure she's alright, my mum would.'

'We need to sneak up there again and see what he's doing,' I said. 'If there is a girl there, we need to make sure that she's alright.'

'But if he catches us again, we'll be in deep trouble.'

'We can't tell the adults what we think yet; they'd only say that we were being silly.'

'Let's tell Jake what we're doing then, if we don't come back, he can raise the alarm.'

It seemed like a good plan. We found Jake and told him what was going on. 'Course I will,' he said, 'I'll follow you and stay out of sight. If he appears, I'll make a lot of noise.'

We crept closer, the caravan's door and all the windows were closed and covered, even though it was a hot day. We both had sticks this time, just in case. We both jumped when there was a sound from inside. Then there was another, a different one. 'Is that what I think it is?' whispered Maisie.

'We have to involve adults now,' I said, shocked at what I'd heard. As we crept back towards the swings; I realised that things were serious. 'Best we don't tell Jake anything. He doesn't need to get involved. My dad will know what to do.' Maisie had been quiet, unusual for her. 'I hope so,' she said.

Jake was waiting for us, 'are you both OK,' he asked, concern in his voice.

'We're fine thanks,' we said, 'it's alright, there was nothing there, it wasn't what we thought.'

He looked dubious, 'you sure?'

'Yes, everything's fine, he just wants to be left alone, it's all OK.' I tried to sound sincere, he needed to keep well away until my dad could sort it all out.

~ ~ ~ ~

'But Dad, you have to listen.' It was two hours later, and we weren't getting anywhere. Perhaps we were explaining it all wrong. Tea had been forgotten as we both tried to get Dad to do something.

'You want me to believe that there's a man in that caravan who's got a girl prisoner?' he said. 'And he's told you to keep away. Have you been annoying him?'

'Yes. No. He has and we haven't. Jake says he's on his own but there was someone else with him, I saw them at the window. Then we saw him in town, buying children's medicine and tee shirts and those tablets that mum has to help her sleep.'

He shot her a look, 'Don't ask,' she said.

'And we went up there again, just now,' I repeated. 'We heard a child crying, he shouted at her to shut up.'

'Right,' he said, 'you've told me the same story three times now. I'm starting to believe you, if you were making it up it would change every time you repeated it. I'm going over there to talk to him. I'm responsible for you and your friend. If you really were doing no harm; he shouldn't speak to you like that. As for the child....,' he didn't say what he thought.

I didn't like the idea of him going up there, knocking on the door. 'He's dangerous Dad, he threatened us.'

34

'Don't you think we ought to call the police?' said Mum, looking worried.

'Very well, I'll call the experts.' He got up, 'there's a phone down by reception.'

He came back ten minutes later, 'they're on the way,' he said. 'They weren't too keen, I had to mention my old job, prove that I wasn't just some random caller. That seemed to change their minds. And when I mentioned a girl as well, for some reason that really got them moving.'

'What did you do at work? Andorra never says much about it.' asked Maisie. Dad smiled, 'I was in the Army, for a while I worked for the government, in the Foreign Office. I worked in British Embassies abroad, helping stranded tourists and that sort of thing. Now, I'm just an events planner.' He was being modest, bless him, he had been the Ambassador, the Countries representative. We had been told not to say too much about what he used to do, for once I had managed to keep my mouth shut. Now that she knew, I could tell her about it later, when this was over.

'Didn't you ought to go to the gate, direct the police in?' Mum asked.

Dad nodded, 'I suppose so.'

While we waited for them, we went outside and watched the corner of the woods where the caravan was.

Dad had only been gone a moment when I saw a load of lights come on, heard a car engine start.

'He must have heard us,' said Maisie, 'now he's running away.'

'We have to stop him,' I went back inside and grabbed Dad's car keys.

'What are you doing Andorra?' asked Mum.

No time to tell her, no time to lose, I'd thought of a way to stop him. I opened the car, sat in the driver's seat and pulled off the handbrake. Before I could shut the door, the car rolled down the little ramp and blocked the lane. Actually, it did more than that, it picked up quite a bit of speed as I tried to put my foot on the brake. My legs weren't long enough to reach it properly, the back of the car hit a tree on the other side. It jolted me out of the seat and sounded awfully loud.

Mum screamed. 'What have you done Andorra?' She was angry, or scared; all red-faced and wild-eyed. She grabbed me, 'are you crazy?'

'He was getting away,' I said, 'now he can't.'

Dad reappeared. 'Are you alright, I heard a scream?' Then he saw his car. 'What on earth has happened. How did that get there?'

Before anyone could speak, we were dazzled by the lights of the old car, towing its caravan, headed our way. He wasn't going anywhere and screeched to a halt about two feet away. The driver blew his horn. We ignored him. 'Stay close to me,' said Dad.

The scruffy man got out of his car, 'shift your heap of junk,' he said, 'I'm in a hurry.'

'No,' said Dad, 'unless you tell me why you threatened my daughter and her friend.'

'They were snooping around,' he replied, 'poking their noses in where they shouldn't.'

Suddenly, a knife was in his hand, Mum screamed again, he waved it about, 'just shift it, unless you want to be wearing this.'

'I can hardly shift it; if I'm bleeding everywhere,' said Dad, calmly.

Just then, there were more lights, from the opposite direction. And a siren.

The man turned and ran away.

A police car stopped; two policemen got out. 'Are you the person who called?' one asked. 'I am,' said Dad pointing them towards where the man could just be seen running across the field, towards the woods. They set off in pursuit. Another police car arrived, what had Dad said?

'What's going on?' one of this car's occupants asked. He was dressed in a suit, the woman with him was in uniform. 'I'm detective Harris, would you be Mr Pett?'

'That's right,' said Dad, holding out his right hand. The policeman shook it. 'My daughter thinks that the owner of this car was holding a girl hostage,' Dad said. The policewoman left us and went into the caravan, the curtains were pulled back and the windows opened, the smell that came out was appalling.

'There's nobody here,' said the policewoman as she came back out, holding a small tee-shirt, 'but there was a girl here, there are clothes and things. Lots of tranquillisers, enough to keep someone half-asleep for ages.'

'Then where is she? The man ran off on his own.'

'In the car?' I suggested.

'Good idea, well done,' said the policewoman. She opened the boot of the car. I saw a girl tied up, unconscious.

She was lifted carefully out and laid on the grass. The policewoman pulled the tape away from her mouth. The girl woke up, panic in her eyes, her speech was slurred

'Are we there yet?' she asked.

'Are you Isabella Forbeson?' asked the policewoman.

'Yes,' she nodded, 'what's happening to me? Has that horrible man gone?'

'You're quite safe, these two girls found you.'

She was crying, 'it was awful, he kept feeding me this revolting drink, it made me feel half asleep all the time, I was sick a lot and every time I woke up, I had a different shirt on.'

'Isabella Forbeson?' said Dad. 'I know her father, Lord Forbeson, the politician.'

That's right Mr Pett, sir. Isabella was kidnapped, a week or so ago,' the detective explained. 'It's been kept a secret, when you called to say you thought a girl was being kept in a caravan, we figured it might be her. We've had a lot of crank calls but when the former ambassador to Argentina calls up, we take notice.'

Maisie looked at me, 'is that why your sister's called Argentia?' I nodded, 'and I'm Andorra for the same reason.'

She giggled again, 'you're cleverer than her then, she can't even spell her name properly.'

Wait till I saw Tia, I bet she'd wish that she'd stayed here with me. But then Maisie wouldn't have come. Rescuing a hostage wouldn't have been half as much fun without her. Tia would have tried to take all the credit, for one thing.

The two policemen arrived, puffing from chasing the man. He was handcuffed and they held him between them. He saw us and pulled a face. 'Bloody interfering kids,' he snarled as they put him in the back of their car. Nobody told him off for saying 'bloody'.

'Take no notice,' the detective said, 'you were very clever and did exactly the right things. I expect Isabella's father will want to thank you properly later.'

'It was unlucky for him,' said the policewoman, 'that you were here.' She pointed at the back of his car, 'anyway, he had an unlucky number plate.'

'What do you mean?' asked Mum.

'Well, number thirteen, that's an unlucky number,' she said. There was a pause, she looked puzzled. 'Why are you all laughing?'

'Um,' said Maisie, between giggles.

Marigold and the Tea-Ladies
By Maura Beckett

'We can't let just anyone join our ranks; you know. We have standards to maintain. The Prixwood Tea-Ladies are a tradition, which I am charged to protect,' exclaimed Sarah Longthorpe, chairwoman of the group.

'I know,' Marigold stammered, 'but I think I'm up to the task. My Victoria Sandwich medalled at last year's Country Fayre.'

'It's not just the baking, you know, we need to ensure all our ladies share a certain etiquette. We have noticed your abilities and would like to offer you a chance to see if you can fit in with us next Sunday. Be at the Village Hall 10am sharp.'

'Oh, thank you so much,' Marigold gushed, 'I won't let you down.'

'No, you won't. If you're not up to scratch, we won't be inviting you back,' Sarah replied. Marigold was not sure if it was a threat or just a statement, but she didn't care.

'I'll see you on Sunday,' she said, leaving with a spring in her step.

Joining the Prixwood Ladies was a big coup for Marigold. She'd arrived in the village five years ago but was still considered something of an interloper. Her husband, Jerry, had told her not to bother however she loved baking and wanted to share her talents with others. She hurried back to her home and crashed through the front door.

'Jez, Jez, are you here?'

'Upstairs, everything ok?'

'Yes, wonderful. You won't believe what just happened. I've got it. Sarah Longthorpe is going to give me a trial, this Sunday.'

'Fantastic, but the hoops she wants you to go through just to be a volunteer are stupid.'

'I know but I just want to fit in and belong.'

'We already do. People always call me if they have a plumbing emergency and you do almost everyone's hair,' he replied.

'And now, I'm a Tea-Lady, too.' Marigold smiled to herself and passed into the kitchen, her favourite place, to make a start on her efforts for Sunday. It was Wednesday already, and she wanted to have a bit of a practice before making the final batches.

She glanced around the kitchen; old but serviceable. Marigold loved it; it was why they had bought the house. Nowadays, it would be called 'shabby chic' but it was, in fact, just old. The estate agent had said it was in need of some work however, five years later, it had come back into fashion all by itself. She opened the tall, pantry door, waiting for the creak. In the beginning it had annoyed her but over the years she had grown accustomed to it, even finding it comforting. Perusing the shelves, she looked over the ingredients, only the best would do for today. She selected her finest grade flour, caster sugar and real, unsalted butter. These scones would be the best Sarah Longthorpe had ever tasted.

Two hours later, Jez peered through the door.

'How's it going?'

'Great. I've made three batches. Now I just I need a tester.'

'No need to ask me twice,' he said, crossing the room and making a pass at the first plate.

'You need to try one from each plate, I want to know which are the fluffiest and have the most flavour.'

'Righty-ho, here goes.' Wiping the crumbs from his mouth, Jez took the plates and rearranged them.

'I feel like a judge from The Bake Off,' he said, getting ready to deliver his verdict. 'In third place are these, a little denser than the rest, there's not much in it between the other two. If I had to pick, I'd go for these,' he pointed to a square plate, 'but they are all amazing.'

'Thanks, I hope they are good enough.'

'Sweetie, they should be pleased to have you, and if they're not, well then they can...you know, get lost.' Marigold gave her husband a kiss.

'I know you think I'm mad, but I'll be accepted and belong once I'm a Tea-Lady. Right, out of my kitchen. I need to make my medal winning Victoria Sandwich, now.'

Sunday morning came and Marigold was up with the lark. The butterflies in her stomach were going mad, it's like there's a kaleidoscope of them in there, she thought.

'Have a cup of tea, help you relax,' came the voice of Jez, cutting through her thoughts.

'Sorry, I was miles away. Good idea, I'm shaking,' she said, holding out her hand and taking the tea, 'how can I be this nervous, it's ridiculous.'

'You'll be great, your baking is excellent, and I'll be in later to see how it's going.'

'Well, it's a quarter to, I'd best be off,' she said, draining the last of her tea. She picked up her cakes and headed out of the door. 'Catch you later.' She closed the door behind her and made her way to the car. Loading it was akin to a game of Tetris. She re-arranged the boxes about twenty times until she was happy that her precious cargo was safe. The short journey to the hall was uneventful but Marigold drove at a snail's pace, fearful of damaging her wares and sabotaging her trial before she'd even got there.

Relief abounded as she arrived at the venue unscathed. Unloading her boxes, she walked into the hall.

'Hello, everyone,' she said meekly, as she arrived. All of the ladies turned around. Most smiled. A youngish, portly lady made her way over and looked as if she was about to speak when the room was distracted by the arrival of their leader. Sarah Longthorpe emerged.

'Ah, good. You can set up with Lucy, here. Everyone,' she said to the room at large, 'this is Marigold, our newest potential member. Let's show her the ropes, what it takes to be a Prixwood Tea-Lady.' Marigold turned to Lucy and smiled, 'Hello.'

'Come with me, I'll show you around.' Lucy said, smiling back. 'Don't take too much notice of her, we all just tolerate her. She loves lording it over us.'

'Do you all feel the same? Why don't you say anything to her?'

'What cross her? We'd be out before our feet had time to touch the ground. No, keep your head down when she's around. The rest of the time we have a good laugh.'

Marigold had been to the village hall on many occasions but never had been allowed behind the big, wooden door to the sanctum behind. Carrying her cakes, she placed them on the closest table and followed Lucy. The kitchen was a hive of activity. It was so different to the old, decrepit facility she had expected. It looked more like an industrial kitchen; stainless steel worktops and cupboards along three of the walls, a huge oven and gigantic fridge on the last. If she hadn't known better, she would have thought she'd walked into a professional restaurant. 'Wow, this is amazing,' she said.

'I know,' Lucy replied, 'we raised the money to refurbish it a few years ago. Sarah is very particular about which groups can use it. I work over there; we all have our own spaces. You can set up here, right next to me.'

'Thanks,' Marigold said, feeling more relaxed in Lucy's company, she was nice.

'Right, ladies,' Sarah's voice bellowed across the room, 'as soon as your cakes are ready let's get the hall set up.' Lucy turned to Marigold,

'Once you've finished topping your scones, we need to go next door. Are you ok?'

'Yes, I'm just finishing up and then I'll be in,' she said, brandishing a pair of teaspoons and pots of jam and Devon clotted cream.

Her task completed, Marigold wiped her hands on a tea cloth and left the kitchen. In the hall, the trestle tables were laid out around the room. Each table required a tablecloth, cups and saucers, plates, cutlery, jams, sugar and a small vase of cut flowers. The look was old-fashioned high tea.

'We each have our own task, mine and now yours as well, is cutlery. We need to make sure each setting has a butter knife, cake fork and teaspoon. We all work around each table. It's really very quick,' Lucy said. Before she knew it, Marigold heard Sarah clapping, calling the room to attention (again).

'This is it, ladies. Action stations.' The main door was opened and the customers swarmed in. Marigold couldn't believe how many people had queued up. There must have been forty people now sat expectantly at the tables. She returned to her area to await instruction.

'We'll work together today; I'll take the orders and you can help bring it over.' Lucy explained as she walked over to her first table. Marigold picked up her beautiful scones, ready to take them over on Lucy's command. Even if she said so herself, they looked magnificent. Just as fluffy, if not more-so than everyone else's. She was so caught up in her self-congratulatory thoughts that she missed the huge intake of breath.

'What are you doing? You can't serve those!' Sarah Longthorpe hissed.

'Pardon. What do you mean?'

'Where are we?'

'Prixwood Village Hall,' Marigold said, in confusion.

'Yes, and in which county is Prixwood?'

'Devon.' She was aware of all eyes in the hall looking at them. 'What's wrong?'

'What's wrong, is that you have prepared Cornish scones, not Devon ones, you idiot.' Sarah looked like she was almost spitting with rage. 'We can't have people with such a huge disregard for tradition in our ranks, please leave.'

'Surely, you're joking.' Marigold said, looking around the room for support. 'I can change them.' The room fell silent, people looking at the floor while Sarah stared at her. Marigold could feel her cheeks reddening, she wasn't sure if she wanted to cry or scream.

'I have worked hard all week to bake some wonderful cakes for today. How dare you tell me that I have to leave.' She didn't have a chance to say anything more before she saw Jez arrive. He looked at Marigold.

'What's wrong?' The room was still quiet.

'Apparently, I'm not welcome here because I made my scones incorrectly.'

'Pardon? How's that?'

'I don't know.'

'In Devon, we always spread cream, then jam. Anyone who can't get that right is not one of us ' Sarah Longthorpe chirped.

Jez was about to open his mouth when Marigold took him by the hand. She shook her head.

44

'All I wanted was to belong, to be a Tea-Lady but if this is what it's like, I don't want to be one of you.' She turned to leave. Everyone was still looking at her. She made her way to the door and turned to see Sarah smirking.

'And you can take that self-satisfied smile off your face,' she said, picking up a scone off her plate and launching it at Sarah. 'Hope you enjoy your Cornish scone,' she said, as it landed right on target.

Puffball
By Chip Tolson

Franklyn couldn't sleep lying shivering on the sofa, the heavy wooden ended piece of furniture he'd cracked his knee against in the dark. He ended up on the floor seeking warmth from Angus stretched out beside him.

Angus had turned, snarling on the cottage threshold, defending his territory. Eager enough to get into the car when Franklyn picked him up, with the keys, from the late owner's niece in Bristol, his mood changed when they'd found the cottage, hidden in the dark depths of Exmoor's night. It was only by digging out a feeding bowl and the bag of biscuits the niece had stuffed into the car's boot that he could distract the spaniel long enough to gain entry to the cottage. Once Angus decided Franklyn was to be the source of food, the stranger's presence was accepted. The cottage had been the dog's home for all his three years from puppyhood until uprooted to the strange city life of past months.

The morning dawned in disappointment, if dawn was the right concept for the damp grey light creeping into Franklyn's temporary home. The ancient kitchen hob produced no hiss of gas to ignite, even if the matches had been dry. It was raining and he had no wet weather gear. A month ago, unemployed and sitting alone in his Chiswick flat, the prospect of several months in a Devon country cottage, paying no rent, tasked by a friend of a friend he'd met in a pub, only with looking after the place, had sounded idyllic.

He'd planned to stop at a supermarket as he'd motored down to Devon, but the journey had dragged on. Victoria's car, the car he'd promised, but failed, to sell for her after she'd departed to New York, had of late only been driven on short journeys in London making trips from their shared flat to the recycling centre under the flyover, clearing the flat of the accumulation of their years together, making it tidy enough to let out.

A prompt expedition from his temporary cottage home to find a food shop was essential; he made a shopping list and... the car wouldn't start. The engine turned over without firing into life, its churning rattle slowing. He was stranded, in a ramshackle cottage with no neighbours, with a dog, in woodland bordered by unknown moorland, on a day of heavy rain.

Searching through dank kitchen cupboards he found two tins, one of sardines, the other of baked beans. These, eaten cold, were all the meal he would have that day in the semi-darkness of Exmoor's rain.

His second wakeful night was little better than his first until he woke to sunlight streaming in through cobwebbed windows. He let Angus out and was amazed when the car spluttered into life with the first turn of the ignition.

A camping shop in South Molton, with a range of sleeping bags, boots and waterproofs designed for wilderness trekkers, solved one problem, a supermarket to stock the cottage's larder solved the other.

~ ~ ~ ~

Franklyn missed Victoria, away on a year's work exchange with her company's New York partners. As a couple they'd been together for four years, true there had been a lot of bickering of late but he'd been steadfast waving her goodbye on her departure from Heathrow, trusting it was a temporary thing, even if it was to be for twelve months. They'd talked of meeting up in the

States when she was due a work break to go on a Road Trip, once every young person's dream. The reality was that Franklyn felt the distance between them when he'd tried to keep in touch. She was always too busy, at work or socially. And he hadn't told her he'd been made redundant from the only employment he'd had since he'd left school more than eighteen years ago. He'd worked steadily up the hierarchy, earning a good salary, his opinions respected and making important trips abroad for the company, all that was before the takeover. New owners and new rules, then a rapid second company sale to Russian owners changed everything.

Not only was he redundant, but he'd found out he was out of the job market loop, mid-thirties with no degree or other special training outside his job experience. His job search became demoralising, his applications unacknowledged. It became difficult keeping contact with Victoria, the opportunity to tell her about losing his job was never there, emails and texts lingered, time differenced phone calls were seldom convenient for one or other party.

As the days following those first two cold nights passed, man and dog built an understanding working around the cottage and making expeditions through the surrounding woodland, then out over the moors, ranging further day by day, in to country unknown to Franklyn yet familiar to the dog, always running ahead, looping back to be sure he was following.

The generator in an outside shed was a challenge. It was not until he found two jerry cans to fill and bring home with a fresh supply of diesel that Franklyn coaxed the machine into life. Even then, the power produced in the cottage was modest. He was more successful, after struggling to lift the waist high empty LPG bottle into the car and, with greater difficulty, Victoria's hatchback groaning on its suspension, heaved the replacement full bottle into place and connected to the gas pipe feeding the cooker; he enjoyed his first hot meal at the cottage.

There was one feature adjoining the cottage that worked well, not surprising since the co-inheritor of the aunt's cottage, her nephew Robert, worked in IT abroad on a long-term contract in the Middle East. This was the communications shed, set up without National Park planning consent, in a wooden hut inside an adjacent stone barn. The building had solar panels on its roof working in conjunction with a wind turbine to charge batteries linked to high performance broadband through a satellite dish.

Night after night, fascinated by starlit skies, Franklyn sat out wrapped in a thick sweater realising how contaminated the London night sky had become disfigured by lights killing all sky vision. Here in darkest Exmoor there was no night time light for miles around the cottage. Franklyn was no astronomer, but he knew how to pick out the occasional planet and, on many evenings, watched the International Space Station making its transit over Europe, getting into the habit of checking its trajectory on the internet.

As was the dog's wont, he was ranging ahead on their way home through the woodland when Franklyn heard excited barking. Thinking Angus was challenging the old man; a strange character who stalked about the woods in a mud-stained ex-army greatcoat and battered bowler hat, Franklyn ran to catch up. Whenever they saw him, Angus snarled keeping his distance. Franklyn had tried to be sociable, but the old man never uttered a word, making off through the trees.

When Franklyn caught up with Angus there was no old man to be seen. The dog was confronting a puffball growing at the edge of a clearing, a place where they'd often paused on the way back from their expeditions. Angus was working himself into a state, growling his challenge, teeth bared and eyes aflame.

'It's a puffball, Angus. Don't tell me you've never seen a puffball. Let's have a kick-about.' Then thinking it would be good to eat the puffball for breakfast next morning, Franklyn laughed at the dog's antics and set off home having to drag Angus away from the clearing.

On a late October morning, six weeks after Franklyn's arrival, everything felt good; he'd slept well in his sleeping bag, he was warm and he was going out to bring home the puffball, to slice it, fry it with bacon, set poached eggs on it and have a slap-up breakfast; recreating a memory of childhood breakfasts with his father.

Savouring the morning mist dancing on cobwebs through the autumn leaved trees, armed with a kitchen knife, Franklyn strode off, laughing at the dog coming only as far as the cottage gate.

In the clearing, Franklyn looked around perplexed. Could this be the same growth that had spooked Angus last evening? It was twice the size. It had to be yesterday's puffball, now the size of a basketball; last evening it had been the size of a supermarket melon. He'd expected it would grow if he left it, but not so fast. It was as big a puffball as he'd ever seen, white, an almost perfect sphere. If it could grow that much overnight what would happen if he left it to grow on for a few more days?

Franklyn trudged back to the cottage empty-handed.

It was time to get the cottage stocked up with provisions for the winter. If he got on with the job he could get back to the cottage and have an afternoon hike. Angus preferred to come with him in the car than to be left on his own. He'd been shut in the house after the old woman's demise. The postman found them, having delivered for three days to the mail box down by the lane, on the fourth day he thought it odd her post was piling up.

It was easy parking at the supermarket; he'd forgotten his list left on the kitchen table, but thought he'd filled his trolley with most of what he needed as he worked the basket load through the bleeping self-service checkout.

A man was standing by Victoria's car staring in at Angus.

'You got Miss Cheverton's dog, then?'

Franklyn looked at his questioner.

'T'is Angus, isn't it, Angus from Westercombe? I know him from when he were a puppy.'

'Yes, it's Angus.' The dog standing on the seat wagging his tail appeared to know the man.

'You the nephew, then?'

'I'm a friend of his looking after the cottage for a while.'

'She were a good sort, Miss Cheverton. Kept herself to herself, mind, but what she didn't know about the country around those parts and the old mine workings, isn't worth knowing.'

'Are you from that area?'

'I was born in those parts; house is gone now. I worked for her father when I were a lad; I lives with me daughter down here now. She'll be missed will Miss Cheverton; saw her last backend, taken sudden folk say.'

A woman at a nearby car called over as she piled shopping into the boot of her car. The old man turned and walked away.

Driving back into the hills Franklyn realised he knew little about the woman whose cottage he'd moved into, living amongst her possessions. It didn't look as if much had been taken away. He guessed she'd lived a frugal life, on her own after her parents died, spending her days walking with her dogs over the moors, no doubt many dogs passing on before young Angus's day,

'Tell me about your Mistress, Angus. I want to know who she was and what she did. I bet she took you out on the moors many times.'

Franklyn looked into the diving mirror, craning his head trying to see the unresponsive dog stretched out along the back seat, uninterested in the topic.

'I'll stack the shopping, Angus then we can go out.'

With the shopping piled on the kitchen table, Franklyn determined to learn more of Miss Cheverton, or 'Aunt Mavis' as the niece in Bristol called her. In a drawer of a mahogany bureau Franklyn found notebooks, more log books than diaries, of the happenings around Westercombe Cottage; lists and dates, of places and things, of birds and animals, of the flowering of plants and shrubs, all written in a small, clear hand.

Angus grew impatient pushing his muzzle against Franklyn's leg as he sat absorbed delving into the privacy of the aunt's life. Page after page in the notebooks the aunt had made a record of her walks, even the rabbits she had shot around the cottage. The number of shot rabbits seemed excessive for rabbit pies, unless she fed her dogs on their meat.

'Alright Angus, let's go out.'

It was too late to go up to the clearing when they ran back to the cottage, rain setting in for the evening. In the doorway, Angus shook sending a fine spray of muddy water onto the door jambs. Franklyn pulled off his damp sweater; he'd not expected rain. He fed Angus, decided he wouldn't do battle with the generator, lit a paraffin lamp found in the barn and used the gas to cook himself an omelette.

Later Franklyn sat down to read through Miss Cheverton's notebooks. There was one giving a full description of a set of mine workings, one of the ancient mines worked in Tudor times on the high moors.

When he took Angus out before bedtime the rain had eased, leaving a crisp night for star gazing, enhanced with an almost full moon rising in the east. On a whim, Franklyn started away from the cottage toward the clearing in the woods. Angus walked with him a distance, snuffling in the undergrowth, then laid down refusing to go further.

Franklyn didn't need a torch to locate the puffball, it was obvious on the far side of the clearing, not only grown still larger, but its silky white, almost luminescent circumference marking it out from its surroundings. He gazed at it wanting to go closer, but uncertain. It looked out of place, an intruder in the woodland clearing.

Franklyn turned back to the cottage breaking into a run as a rain cloud eclipsed the moon. Angus, waiting at the garden gate, greeted him circling around before they rushed together into the house.

In the early morning, with the half-light breaking through leafless trees, Franklyn was back in the clearing. His mind had ranged over the peculiarity of the fungal growth much of the night. There was an obvious glow from the puffball like some creature of the deep ocean, generating its own light. It had grown to considerable size.

Back at the cottage after a fried breakfast, he went to the hut in the stone barn, opened his laptop and set about an internet search. There had to be an explanation, even if this fruit was not a puffball usually found in Britain. Maybe it was a jungle growth that through strange circumstance had come to Devon, escaped from a collector's fungatorium or, like sand from the Sahara, its spores had been carried out of Africa on high altitude currents. It couldn't be native to Devon.

One after another, websites showed all sorts of fungi growing in countries around the world from the arctic circle to the tropics, from arid lands to jungles. Puffballs could be small or very big, he discovered *Calvatia Gigantica* can grow to a three-foot diameter. At the rate his puffball was growing, it would be a match, yet there the similarity stopped, there was no mention of any luminous glow from fungi fruit, whatever their size, and there were none that showed such symmetry in their growth. Search as he might there was nothing recorded on the web to match his giant.

Angus was pushing a paw against Franklyn's leg wanting to be out on the moors. 'Soon, Angus, we'll be off soon.'

An internet entry caught his eye from a blog, written in English by a person in Japan. Ito Hirasawa, a retired Professor of Botany, resident in Kyoto, told how on a regular basis he trekked in the mountains reporting on botanic sightings. There was a note of excitement in his latest commentary. He'd found two puffballs, one bigger and older than the other, both growing at great pace. They were symmetrical and at dusk appeared to have a luminous glow. He'd had no camera with him on the day he'd found the fungi and hadn't had the chance to get back up to the site; he hoped to post a photo soon.

Franklyn sat staring at his laptop. This had to be the same thing, it was the sole reference to anything similar to his puffball.

'This is it, Angus. We've found a sibling puffball.'

Angus put his head on one side, gave a bark and went to the door.

'Five minutes, Angus, I must put a comment on this blog, tell the Professor about our puffball. Then we'll go out.'

Franklyn thought back to his business visits to Japan. Eight hours, or so, ahead in time, mid-afternoon in England, the middle of the night in Japan. He wrote a comment on the blog:

Professor Hirasawa, I live in the United Kingdom and have observed a puffball with the same characteristics you are describing for the two puffballs near Kyoto.

This puffball is sited in a clearing of deciduous woodland on Exmoor, Devon, England, at approximately 900 feet above sea level. I will take a photo and post it later today.

I am FRANKLYN THOMALIN, living temporarily about a quarter of a mile from the puffball location. Regards.

'Come on, Angus we have work to do and no fuss from you, please. We need photos of our puffball.'

~ ~ ~ ~

Franklyn cut short their ramble on the moor determined to get back to the puffball with his camera before daylight faded.

Professor Ito Hirasawa had been at his computer at an early hour in Kyoto. Hirasawa's reply to his comment on the blog stressed how unusual the puffballs were. The professor was keen to see any photograph to confirm similarities and promised he would add photos of the Japanese fungi as soon as he could, warning there was a storm headed for the Kansai region.

Franklyn had marked up a measuring stick with rounds of black tape at six-inch intervals. Having taken his first photos, he'd stuck the marked stick in the ground beside the puffball to take further shots.

He hadn't eaten since breakfast; he put Angus out of his impatience with a bowl of dog biscuits, he boiled a kettle for coffee. In the barn hut, he downloaded his pictures onto his laptop.

He selected two, one taken with the flash and the other without, showing the measuring stick beside the spherical growth glowing in the fading light. These two pictures he added, with further comment, on to Hirasawa's blog. He then sent a separate email to the professor attaching an album of puffball pictures. It was nine o'clock UK night time, five in the morning in Kyoto. His coffee was cold.

Next morning, there was nothing from Japan, but there was a comment from a person in Chile. He reported seeing a large round puffball, four weeks back that appeared to be luminescent; when he'd passed by the same place two days later it had burst.

'Angus, there is another one in South America.'

The dog, dozing, opened one eye, giving a modest flick of his tail.

Hirasawa came back by email excited by the photos, certain the puffballs in the UK and Japan were the same unrecorded species: he could think of no reason for them to appear at the same time in Europe and in Japan. And if the report from Chile stood up to verification a greater question would hang in the air.

The South American correspondent, a research student working in the foothills of the Andes, confirmed his sighting was of a similar opaque puffball as in the photographs, he reported it growing to about a metre in diameter before bursting to a split skin. Then Georgi Ivanovich, living north of Omsk, reported he had seen a similar growth in his work in the northern forests of Russia, ending as a vacated skin. Next there was a report from a doctor working in the Guyanan rain forest, and later a reindeer herder in Finland, all reporting similar sightings.

On a star-studded late October evening Franklyn sat outside with his thick coat buttoned up, a bottle of local beer in his hand, watching the Space Station cross the early night sky, at the time and on the course stated on the website. As the reflected sunlight from the craft transiting the eastern sky faded, somewhere over the Baltic States, Franklyn returned to the warmth of the log fire; his time sawing firewood amply rewarded. He sat studying a world map he'd found in a dusty atlas plotting the locations of the reported puffball sightings.

The thought struck him, a flowing line could be drawn connecting the reported sightings, a line that bore similarity to the ground track of orbiting satellites. Unable to contain his excitement Franklyn emailed Hirasawa in Kyoto.

In the UK morning, Franklyn skyped Hirasawa to discuss the number of puffball reports. Hirasawa took up Franklyn's suggestion of a pattern in the reported sightings; they conjectured possible implications, even the thought there might be some extra-terrestrial source. Professor Hirasawa told Franklyn, his hesitant English tumbling words together in his excitement, the first puffball he had been observing had split open without trace of its contents. He planned to cut open the second growth on site.

Franklyn urged caution; they agreed a plan. Hirasawa would make contact using his mobile at the puffball site. They fixed a time; noon the next day Japan time, four a.m. in Devon, for Hirasawa to work on the puffball while calling Franklyn.

That night the phone didn't ring until half past four in the morning; Hirasawa, in a confused call, said he was unable to get a signal at the puffball site. He was certain there was movement, a pulse, inside the puffball. He was going back to the site and would ring again in an hour.

There was no further call.

~ ~ ~ ~

At midday, already evening in Kyoto, Franklyn tried to contact Hirasawa. There was no answer; he left messages on his mobile, on his home landline and on the blog. Hours later Hirasawa's wife made contact through a family friend who spoke hesitant English. Her husband had gone missing; a search party had been organised.

Franklyn left Angus at the cottage gate running to his puffball site to find only the shrivelled skin in its place... and nearby the old man's bowler hat lying on the ground. A few yards away Franklyn spotted the first growth of a second puffball, tennis ball sized.

On an impulse, Franklyn decided he had to go to Kyoto to meet with Hirasawa's wife and colleagues. He had cash in the bank now the rent for the Chiswick flat was coming in; he booked himself onto a flight to Osaka from Heathrow, checked his passport, packed a small bag and went early to bed. Angus was puzzled by the change of routine, even more so in the morning when he was delivered back to Bristol as children were getting ready for school.

'I can't have the dog back.'

Franklyn was already at the garden gate. 'I'm parked on double yellows. I'll pick him up in a few days.'

Thirty-six hours later, Franklyn, exhausted from his journey, arrived in Kyoto. Despite three days of searching no trace of Hirasawa's whereabouts had been found. Franklyn spent days and nights with the professor's colleagues visiting places where Hirasawa was known, all to no avail.

Back in the UK, reunited with Angus in the Exmoor cottage, Franklyn maintained contact with others around the world who'd reported sightings, updating them on Hirasawa's disappearance, and the explosion of his own Exmoor puffball.

There were no additional reports of puffball sightings. Franklyn's second puffball, now growing to larger dimensions, visibly luminescent in the winter daylight, with its throbbing pulse clear to see, presented an ominous threat. Having read in the notebooks of the rabbits Miss Cheverton had shot, Franklyn searched the cottage for her shotgun, looking in concealed places, missing the obvious until he saw the shotgun, an ancient BSA bolt action 4:10, propped in a dark corner of the kitchen. In a cupboard, he found cartridges of doubtful vintage.

Franklyn had no expertise with firearms, handling none since he had shot an air rifle at targets in his School Cadet Corps two decades ago.

Standing clear of his target in the woodland clearing, unable to stop his hands shaking, uncertain of the outcome, Franklyn hesitated before the kick back of the shotgun's butt slammed in to his shoulder, hitting his cheek. The puffball exploded into a swirling spore cloud before the wind took it; for a moment he stared at the scene, then turned to run from the clearing as the spores surged toward him.

Franklyn busied himself at his laptop after he and Angus got back from their afternoon walk, establishing there were no reported sightings earlier than in the two months previous to current exchanges. Further internet research turned up that two months before the first report and largely unreported, an asteroid had entered the earth's atmosphere, estimated to have impacted in the South Pacific.

Through November he twice set up skype calls to Kyoto, the first with Hirasawa's colleague, with the professor's wife in the background. Her husband's disappearance was weighing heavily. Nothing new came from the call. On the second occasion, it was one of the professor's ex-students who had taken leave from his employer and was leading the search. He gave an update on the search. They'd found the site of the puffballs, found no new growths, a metal shield and Hirasawa's mobile were lying nearby and there were tracks indicating flight from the scene. Within a hundred yards the trail was lost.

With no further news from Japan and no more reported sightings, life settled into a winter routine of sawing and splitting logs to keep the stoves burning day and night. December set in with every sign of harsh winter weather on the way. Franklyn made occasional trips into town to keep the larder shelves well stocked. He and Angus widened their adventuring, at last finding the location of the Tudor mines noted in Miss Cheverton's notebooks.

It had snowed in the afternoon, Franklyn relaxed in front of the fire with a bottle of wine, shedding his boots to warm his feet. Angus started to growl.

'What's up, Angus. Is the Exmoor Beast coming to get you?'

The dog rose up, hackles standing, growling a deep rumble in his throat. There was thump against the front door. Angus flew across the room.

A body fell into the cottage as Franklyn opened the door, the dog pushed past growling.

'Get away, Angus. Who the hell?'

Franklyn grabbed a torch and turned the body over. The eyes flickered as the wreck of the man tried to speak.

Hirasawa, clutching a battered rucksack, stared up at Franklyn.

~ ~ ~ ~

Over the next few hours Franklyn managed to remove Hirasawa's filthy clothing, to flannel wash his face, clothe him in an old pair of pyjamas with two sweaters, and feed him hot soup. The professor was lying wrapped in blankets on the sofa. He tried to speak, but couldn't master his English, rambling in Japanese. Franklyn was no wiser how the man had got to Exmoor, let alone how he had survived without discovery over the weeks since they'd exchanged telephone calls before his assault on the Kyoto puffball.

The dog wouldn't go near their visitor, a continuing rumbling growl in his throat. Franklyn took Angus to feed him in the communication hut in the barn leaving him there, curled up in his dog-bed, for the night.

Next day Franklyn tended to Hirasawa as the retired professor began to liven up, giving profuse thanks to his host. By the evening Hirasawa was taking steps around the main room and his hunger was building. Franklyn cooked a meal of fish, vegetables, rice and soy sauce, falling well short of any Japanese meal he remembered from his business visits. At last Hirasawa was recovering his voice.

'How did you find your way here, Professor?'

'Franklyn-san, I had all your contact details written in my notebook. I came by plane from Japan, then train, a taxi and a day long walk.'

'But why come here, not to your own home, Professor? Your wife, does she know you have come here?'

Hirasawa shook his head. 'Nobody knows. I am still disappeared in Japan. It is best that way, Franklyn-san.'

'Why?'

'The puffball exploded, I had taken precaution, I had a shield, I expected it to burst, but it still caught me, I was covered in its spores, I failed in my task.'

'Why not seek help... at home, Professor?'

'I washed in a forest stream, but now the puffball spores are inside me. At night I stole fresh clothes from houses near the forest. I know the puffball is in me. It is living in me.'

'I don't understand, Professor. The puffball cannot be living in you. How did you travel, someone must have helped you?'

'Yes, I had help, it was a person who did not know me, Franklyn-san. We had never met before, and will never meet again.'

'I don't understand. Why not go home, Hirasawa-san?'

'I am infected by the puffball. It is inside me, Some alien thing is growing in my body. It is claiming me. You were the only being who would understand my situation. I can trust you, Franklyn-san.'

'Hirasawa-san, this cannot be the truth. Tomorrow I will take you to a hospital for a check-up.'

'I will not go to hospital. It cannot be stopped. I am... as a chrysalis, it is growing inside me, the alien life will burst out and I will be cast off, left empty, a desiccated cadaver. There must be other hosts, wild animals setting off the reported puffballs, and who knows how many more unseen, all nurturing this alien life.'

It transpired the man who had helped, getting him clothes, money, a false passport and his air ticket, was an expatriate Englishman, illegally in Japan for many years. Hirasawa had used the man's laptop to transfer money from a bank account his wife knew nothing of, the Englishman was given a generous payment for his work and to keep silent; it was doubtful his friends in Kyoto would ever find out about his departure from Japan.

'I still don't understand why you are here, Professor, and not at home receiving medical attention.'

'It is best. I cannot be cured. I have dishonoured my family.'

It was going to be impossible to get Hirasawa to a hospital. The next best thing would be to get the professor into better health then seek again to persuade him to return home. For days, they went out in the car, leaving Angus behind. They explored places on Exmoor, in the villages and on the hilltop moors where, if the weather was amenable, they started taking short walks, and soon longer walks as the fresh winter air restored his visitor to better health.

On one day, they reached the ancient mine site identified in Miss Cheverton's notebook. It was fenced off to keep people away from any danger lurking within. On another day, they drove up Countisbury Hill close by Lynmouth, linking up with the South West Coast Path, to look out over the Bristol Channel to Wales from above the lighthouse at Foreland Point.

Franklyn thought it best not to take the professor to the site of his local puffballs, but he took the chance to slip out one evening as Hirasawa dozed after a long drive around Exmoor's narrow lanes. There was no sign of new growth. That evening they ate a meal cooked by Hirasawa to celebrate the New Year. Franklyn had attempted a Christmas lunch the week before, somewhat constrained by the cottage's limited facilities.

'Tell me, Franklyn-san; is your puffball gone, burst open?'

'Yes, and there was a second one, I destroyed it after your accident, Hirasawa-san.'

'How?'

Franklyn grinned, 'with a shotgun I found here. It went up in a great cloud of spores, a huge swirling cloud, then I had to run for it as it was coming my way.'

'Do you suffer after effects?'

'No. The first fruit growing here had burst one night. There has been an old man wandering around in these parts. I found his hat near the burst skin, I guess he had to run for it as well.'

'Have you seen him since?'

'No; that is his bowler hat on the peg by the door. I'm keeping it for when I next see him.'

Hirasawa said nothing, hands shaking, he stood up, reached his unsteady hand to pick up a fire iron to lift the hat from its peg, placing it to burn on the log fire, staring into the flames as the hat was destroyed. The professor turned and bowed to Franklyn. 'We have to find this old man. He will die, the spores are seeded in him as they are in me. We must find him and put him out of his misery.'

'You can't do that, Hirasawa-san.'

'He is dying. We have to find him; it will be a mercy.'

'We don't know that, you don't know... you're... you cannot know it, you are making it up.'

'It is the honourable thing to do.' Hirasawa bowed toward the ashes of the hat. 'When it is my time, I will go also. We will need your shotgun, Franklyn-san.'

'That's ridiculous, Hirasawa-san. Anyway, I haven't got the gun. I handed it in to the police.'

Hirasawa bowed before seating himself cross-legged on the floor in a corner of the room, his arms folded, his eyes shut.

Late that night Franklyn smuggled the shotgun outside, finding a hiding place in the bushes well away from the cottage.

~ ~ ~ ~

Franklyn was woken by Angus barking from the barn. Searching the house, he realised the Professor had disappeared. In a flash he guessed Hirasawa's intent. He pulled on clothes and ran to get Angus.

'No time for biscuits, Angus. We've got to find him.' The dog rushed off into the woodland with Franklyn in pursuit. Even after so many walks and his open-air life style, Franklyn struggled to keep in touch with the dog. After running up and down hills, he had to stop, clutching onto a gate, his lungs aching. Angus came back and looked at him, his tail wagging fit to bust.

'Give me a break, Angus.'

The dog was eager to be off again. Franklyn stood bowed over the gate, his chest heaving, feeling sick.

The dog was away, barking and disappearing through the trees. Franklyn set off, grabbing at trees as he careered down the slope. Breaking out from the wood he found he was at the fenced-off mine entrance. The padlock on the gate was broken, the chain hanging down. Trembling, the dog crept forward in to the mine entrance. Franklyn followed, water dripping from above, far ahead he could see a light flickering.

Growling, Angus stood where the tunnel opened out into a cavern, a lit candle set on a ledge in the rockface threw patterns across the mine wall, on the cavern floor below the furthest reach of the space, there was bundle of clothes. Franklyn edged across making out a familiar ex-army greatcoat, the body within shrivelled, the old man's chest burst asunder revealing an empty cavity. He fled, bile erupting into his mouth.

Franklyn came-to in daylight stretched out on wet grass, Angus licking his face, pushing his muzzle against his cheek. Back at the cottage, Angus froze on the threshold, growling. Franklyn grasped a stout stick, pushed the door open, peering into the gloom. Hirasawa was sitting cross legged in the corner of the room as if unmoved since the night before.

~ ~ ~ ~

Early next morning, hours before dawn, Franklyn woke to the sound of crunching gears. Victoria's car was being driven away. Hirasawa was gone leaving a candle lit beside a note to say he was going to Countisbury Hill to contemplate his fate. Franklyn was stranded. Fetching Angus from the barn, they set off blundering through still dark woodland, yomping in driving rain to the distant main road. Soaking wet and panting, as first light crept into the day, seeing headlights Franklyn flagged down a van. The driver looked at the man and dog, hesitating. Hearing of the stolen car, he agreed to get them to Lynmouth. In the town, Franklyn, handed over a ten-pound note to persuade a taxi driver to take him and the dog to the carpark on Countisbury Hill.

In the teeth of gale force wind Franklyn stood by the taxi in the car park leading to Foreland Point seeing no sign of Victoria's car until a break in the driven rain caught low winter

66

sun reflecting on an object in the distance. The taxi driver shook his head, said he could go no further and drove off. Franklyn and Angus, headed for Victoria's car, following its tracks along a grass path as the rain swept in stinging his face.

The car, slewed across the path, was caked in mud, its wheels axle deep in channels of water. Hirasawa was nowhere to be seen. Angus circled round before picking up a scent leading toward Foreland Point. His heart pumping, Franklyn struggled, feet slipping, along the path. The rain eased as he reached the Coast Path, he shouted out for Hirasawa. Nothing could be heard above the storming wind.

Franklyn crept further along the precipitous path, out over The Foreland toward the lighthouse above the sea. Ahead and far below, close to the edge of the rainswept cliff, he saw a figure; closer still he saw it was Hirasawa, bare headed, bare footed, clad only in a yakata, crouching, rocking back and forward. Franklyn hesitated, watching before shouting again into the wind. Hirasawa stood up tall, with a brief backward glance. He paused, calling into the wind before, with a glint of steel, he swung his arm stabbing into his belly, pulling across his midriff. The storm hushed, all was still, the professor lurched toward the cliff, staggering before his knees buckled, somersaulting into oblivion over the cliff edge.

Franklyn scrambled down to the spot where the professor had stood. A bloodstained carving knife, taken from the cottage, had fallen onto splattered ground, a soaking crimson trail leading over the cliff.

Far below huge waves crashed onto the rocks, Franklyn stared down, mesmerised at the spreading pink pattern in the foaming sea. In a furious spasm Franklyn scooped up the knife hurling it into the sea.

The wind roared, Franklyn giddy with shock, his mind in turmoil, crawled away from the awful scene, his stomach heaving. Somehow, he scrambled back to the abandoned car, slumping down in the heather his mind in torment. Hugging Angus, man and dog shook in distress.

Maybe hours, possibly only minutes later, voices were approaching, two runners working their way along the Coast Path.

'Are you OK, mate?'

'I can't move the car; it was stolen from the car park.'

'Was it locked?

'It doesn't lock.'

The two runners looked at each other. 'You need to get that fixed, mate. We'll see if we can get it out.'

The two men managed to ease the car out of the mud while Franklyn stood by helpless. One of the runners got in backing the vehicle until it could be turned and driven to the car park, Franklyn, supported by the other runner, staggered along the track. He couldn't stop shaking.

'You don't look too good.'

'I overdid it heaving at the car. I'll be all right.'

'You need to be checked over. Get in the back, and your dog, we'll drive you into town. The dog's a quiver and all.'

Franklyn climbed into the back with Angus and the tears came. The two runners sat in the front, the one who'd reversed the car driving. Franklyn lost track of time and place as the men drove.

There was a nurse asking him questions; the two runners, the car and Angus weren't with him.

Three hours later, back at Westcoombe Cottage, Franklyn watched a police 4x4 drive away. Unable to concentrate, the awful visions of past hours swamping his mind, he'd tried to explain to the two uniformed officers - the runners who had rescued him and Angus off the hill - why he was living in the late Miss Cheverton's cottage. He had totally failed to explain about the now impounded vehicle, why he'd been driving an untaxed car, without a valid MOT certificate, registered to an owner resident in Chiswick, said to be living in New York.

The two constables told him they would be checking facts, contacting the car's registered owner and return with more questions.

Franklyn couldn't begin to speak of the horrendous happenings of the past two days. Perhaps he never would speak of those events.

He slumped down on the sofa; Angus climbed up beside him. Franklyn put his arm around the dog, hugging him close.

'Why did he seek us out, Angus? Why would he not go home to Kyoto? He should have gone home. I should have told them he was here. Now I can't tell anyone.' Franklyn shivered and wept.

In a New York office, Victoria put her cell-phone down and stared at her colleague.

'Something the matter, Vicky?'

'That was the police, the UK police in the West of England. They say my fiancé is living rough, in a derelict woodland cottage on Exmoor. He's suffering a break down.'

'You said you both lived in London.'

'I have to go to him. It's urgent.'

Cottage Hospital
By Jenifer Braund

It looked like being a quiet night. Jan and Mary started the night routines; settling patients, putting out commodes. Jan started the medicine round while Mary finished off. The day staff hadn't lingered after report, it was Christmas Eve and everyone wanted to get back to their families. The empty side ward where the afternoon's staff party had been was tidied and armchairs and Christmas fare left for the night staff's Christmas vigil. The Carol singers had been and gone and tomorrow the local dignitaries and league of friends would make their Christmas visit.

Then the senior doctor would carve the turkey for the patient's Christmas Dinner.

Once the day sister had left Jan went down to lock up behind her. It was an old hospital with several external doors and though the porter locked most when he left at six all had to be made secure for the night. Jan the night staff nurse and Mary her auxiliary were the only staff at night for the twenty bed unit and the small Casualty department. She moved from room to room, switching off forgotten lights, checking that the windows were shut fast. One security light was out and would have to wait until after the holiday.

The Day Unit cheerful and still warm with its comfy armchairs showed tidied remains of Christmas festivities. Jan paused looking around almost hearing the cheerful chatter of its dozen or so old folk who visited each day, cared for by nurse supervised volunteers. She knew the unit well. She moved on;

physiotherapy, occupational therapy, chiropody, Casualty, Xray, Admin, through to the small staff dining room and into the kitchens, gleaming and scrubbed. Outer doors and windows secure she was about to return upstairs, when she heard a child crying. A light gleamed faintly from beneath the Casualty doors. Surprised, she tried the door; it yielded. Inside a young man in a suit leaned over a child on the couch. A young woman watched anxiously. The man turned and smiled stethoscope poised,

'Hi, Staff nurse, nearly done, this young lady had a tumble trying to spot Father Christmas,'

He introduced the young Mum and Sally. Jan cleared up as he showed his patient out, then popped his head around the door to say goodnight.

'Bye, have a quiet night, Merry Christmas.'

With that he disappeared and Jan heard the outer door snap shut.

She didn't think any more about it, as Mary phoned down needing help with a restless patient.

'Mrs Liddell is going to keep us busy even though we're only half full.'

There were eleven patients, only four men, so several of the small wards had been shut up, and a side ward made ready in case of an admission.

At last Mrs Liddell was settled. Mary made them both a coffee to ward off any sleepiness. Feet up, Mary tucked into chocolates as Jan peeled a tangerine, then flicked the TV channels to see what was on. 'She Devil' just starting; a thriller just ending, 'Carols from Canterbury.' She settled on the latter turned the sound low and they both put their feet up.

Mary was reading Jan's horoscope when the crash had them both leaping to their feet. The corridor was silent; they strained into the silence listening for bells, calls, clues, nothing. Jan headed for the ladies, Mary to the men. They met up at the top of the stairs perplexed.

'It must be downstairs, there was a patient downstairs Sister forgot to mention, she must have thought they had gone.'

Jan started down the stairs. Mary put out a hand to stop her,

'Hang on Jan, Doctor Peters is on call, he would have come up.'

Jan shrugged, 'It wasn't our lot, they are out on the razzle, and midnight church afterwards.'

She grinned, 'I'd better check downstairs just in case a drunk has chucked a brick in again.'

She disappeared down the stairs. Everything seemed in order the kitchen end. Casualty was locked as she had left it. The sound of carols and cheerful laughter drew her to the Day unit. She frowned, perplexed, snapped lights on and moved down the corridor. Pausing outside the closed door she could hear chattering. She opened the door cautiously, the TV was on, the Canterbury Carols; a dozen people were standing around talking, sipping hot punch and passing around mince pies. One smiled at her, then a phone rang and she moved down the corridor to answer it.

Mary spoke quickly, 'What is going on down there, sounds like a riot'

'You have a casualty coming in, child fallen downstairs, Dr Peters is meeting them here. Are you all right?'

'We have carol singers in the day unit, one of the volunteers must have had a key to the fire escape! I'll get Casualty opened up then come back and see them out. All quiet up there?'

'As a mouse,' Mary chuckled,

'They have left us some wine and I found another box of chocolates your favourite.'

Jim Peters arrived simultaneously with a young woman carrying a little girl. Jan followed them into casualty. Doctor Peters examined the child chuckling and teasing until the little girl managed a tearful smile. He leaned back,

'A bravery sticker I think Staff nurse, and do we have something special as it's Christmas?'

Jan reached into the jar of Christmas teddies.

'This young lady was trying to spot Father Christmas and fell down the stairs.'

Jan was still staring at him as he opened the door to see them out.

'What's up Staff? You look as if you have seen a ghost.'

Jan explained the coincidence. He cut her short,

'We haven't got a locum, he never arrived, so I'm on call! And this is only my second tonight, an hour ago I was out at Back Farm with Mrs Smith and her bronchitis.'

Jan felt vaguely uncomfortable, she shrugged the feeling off.

'Any tea?'

Jim headed for the stairs. Jan nodded,

'I'm just going to check the Day Unit, there's a crowd of carol singers in there.'

She walked down the corridor unaware of Jim Peters staring at her receding back. Slowly he followed her. She pushed the door open all was quiet. The room was empty just as it had been when she locked up earlier. No sign of carol singers, punch, or mince pies. Wide-eyed she looked at the doctor, who was looking carefully around the room. He switched off the TV and the silently mouthing choir.

'They're back' he breathed,

'Fifty years ago carol singers were blamed for the death of a little girl who fell down the stairs thinking they were Father Christmas. She died here in the hospital.'

He stared around the room, 'This would have been Casualty then, the children's ward was where Casualty is. They were nearly all elderly; they died one by one, some of grief, some of natural causes. Eventually, a few years after the last one died they were seen each Christmas Eve. It was said the mother never recovered, she died herself within the year, upstairs!'

He paused, 'Let's get that tea.'

Mary had just done a round, 'Mrs Liddell is asleep at last, she looks really peaceful.'

Jim looked up,

'Mrs Liddell, Briar Cottage?'

Jan nodded,

'She was the child's grandmother, are you sure she's ok?'

Jan and the doctor looked into the ward were the old lady slept, barely visible in the faint light. A child, a young woman and a young man with a stethoscope were beside her bed. Jan snapped her torch on, moving swiftly to the bedside. Only the patient and the bed were caught in the beam of light. She heard Jim's in drawn breath a step behind her.

The old lady was peaceful, still and... dead. Jan drew the curtains.

One of the other patients spoke softly,

'Her family were with her at the end nurse, she was happy.'

'I needed that tea,' Jim grinned, helping himself to a piece of Christmas cake.

'No-one told you about Christmas Eve I see!'

Jan saw Mary grimace,

'No-one will do nights if we tell 'em, and I'm not doing them on my own.'

'But who was the doctor I saw?' Jan asked, still bemused.

Jim pointed to a sepia toned photograph on the office wall. A youngish man stared down at them from an old staff photo dated fifty years ago.

Jan stared into a familiar face... she had seen it twice that night.

The Destiny That Shapes Our Ends
By Brian Willis

Reg Bennett of the 12th Devon Regiment went over the top.

The whistle blew, and over the top he went. In front of him was Corporal Les Harrington, an old pal.

In fact, it was a Pals Regiment, all from the Exmoor village of Nether Arkham.

Reg was the village postman.

Les was the local bobby, the Army top brass, in its wisdom, awarded him the rank of corporal.

A hail of machine-gun fire raked at them; mortar shells exploded above them.

Men all around them were instantly mown down like so much wheat at harvest time.

Shrapnel from an exploding mortar shell caught Les full face, turning it into a bloody maw.

He collapsed into a sodden, stench ridden shell hole, Reg dived in after him.

For Les, mercifully, death was instant. Not for him a primitive plastic surgery face repair back in Blighty. Then, permanent institutionalization, hidden away from public view, as so many were.

Reg landed on the corpse of his friend, he instantly rolled off, recoiling in horror.

In his frantic effort to distance himself from the remains of his friend he collided with something bulky, heavy, and waterlogged, like an oversized bolster, that was slowly submerged in the sludgy reeking water at the bottom of the shell hole.

Reg observed in petrified awareness, that there was gurgling, bubbling sound from this soggy dummy like thing that he stumbled upon.

As he desperately scrambled over this horrific apparition, it rolled over and a grey uniformed arm rose up from the turbid mass. A bearded matted face came into view, a guttural groan emitting from its mouth.

The horror subsided and humanity took over the mind and being of Reg. He grabbed hold of the arm of the German soldier, pulled him upright.

A Guardian Angel, for so thought Reg, (maybe the Angel of Mons) had provided a trench ladder at the edge of the bomb crater.

After what seemed like an endless and superhuman struggle, Reg dragged himself and the enemy soldier out of the flooded death pit.

With the German comatose on the ground, Reg furtively rose to his feet.

He sensed rather than heard a sharp crack above and behind him, a searing pain caught him in his lower back, and he blacked out.

Two weeks later Reg woke from a coma in a field hospital well behind the front line, he had no memory of how he'd got there.

His last memory was of being beside the unconscious German. What became of the enemy soldier nobody could tell him.

The stretcher-bearers who recovered Reg from the battlefield might have been able to, but they were long gone.

A week before, on the eleventh of November 1918, Armistice was declared.

The war to end all wars; was over.

Reg was finally repatriated to Nether Arkham.

Of the twenty-seven Pals that went to the front to fight, only six returned.

Arthur Butt, apprentice blacksmith, twenty-two, would be smithy-ing no more, he was blinded by mustard gas, Ray Stabb the other village Postman would have no use for his post bike, his legs had been amputated.

What of Reg?

He had been shot by an English sniper, who thought he was a German rescuing one of his own.

Reg dragging the German soldier through the water of the bomb crater had washed most of the grime off of the Germans uniform, whereas Reg's uniform was indistinct. Thus, the sniper wrongly assumed that Reg was the enemy too.

The sniper's bullet went through Reg's lower back, left-hand side, damaging his spine.

Although he could walk with a severe limp which gave him pain for the rest of his life, his postman days were over.

However, Reg passed the counter clerk's exam and worked on the post office counter at the main Post office at Higher Arkham, until his retirement.

In 1968 Higher Arkham Legion club organized a coach trip to Germany to visit the 1st world war battlefields to commemorate the 50th anniversary of the end of the 1st world war.

Reg and a former counter clerk colleague Roger Watts, who also was a 1st world war veteran, went on this trip.

After visiting the Somme, Passchendaele, Mons, and other battle sites, the coach went on into Austria, to a small village called Gotzens, overlooking Innsbruck.

There the trippers were to spend a week before returning to England.

Whilst there Reg and Roger chanced to walk in the churchyard of Saint Oswald the martyr, the village Catholic Church.

There they came upon a war memorial to the German fallen of the 1st world war. Sitting on a bench was an elderly gentleman, much the same as them. He was gazing at the memorial in deep thought.

He broke his reverie, glanced up and saw the two English men. He said to them in faultless English with a faint German accent. 'My name is on that memorial'.

'But you're very much alive,' said Reg. 'And I don't believe in ghosts, not even in graveyards,' Roger retorted.

'Let me explain,' said the stranger.

'My name is Hans Liebermann; I was a private in the 1st World War.

I was left for dead on the battlefield, but I was pulled out of a bomb crater by an English soldier, he saved my life.

The Tommy was shot as he stood up and then fell to the ground by the side of me. British stretcher-bearers took both of us back to the British line. We were separated, I made a full recovery, I never saw the Englishman again.

I was interned as a prisoner of war but was released after armistice.

I had no wish to go home, so I went to England to try to find the Englishman that saved my life, but to no avail.

I stayed in England, got a job in London. Met an English girl and got married. This is the first time I've been back home. I still haven't found my English saviour.'

'You have now,' Reg said.

The Old Mill
By Maura Beckett

James clambered up the steep slope and looked. The image was imprinted on his brain. How many times had he visited this spot? It never failed to amaze and delight him. Gentle rolling hills, dotted with trees, interspersed with yellow, shimmering gorse. There, on the farthest hill, stood The Old Mill. A red brick façade, sitting on the bank of the stream. A wheel spinning gently as the water bubbled past.

He hurried there, anticipation filling every part of his body. He felt as if he might explode. Today was the day. The day to change his life. He broke into a sprint, unable to wait any longer. He was ascending the last few steps when he stopped. If today was the day to change his life, what would that mean for his family, his friends and everyone? Could he bear it? The implications were extensive.

He was torn between a life he knew but did not want and the life he could have. As he stood on the hill he was reminded of the enormity of this decision.

James sat. He had been so excited for today that he had pushed all negative thoughts from his mind. The Old Mill held the key to his destiny. The one he loved so desperately was waiting. He longed to be there. As he wrestled once more with his conflicting thoughts James became aware of what he would do. What he had always known he would do. He had been caught up in the romance and excitement. But it was not for him. James was born for other things.

His family had taught him that from the day he was old enough to understand. The privilege he enjoyed had a price; a duty. James had never questioned this; until he met his love.

Suddenly, he had wanted something else. A life like anyone else might have. To be free to work and live and love. Every moment since then had been filled with planning for this day. The day he would take back his life and move on.

But James was not meant for that life. With tears in his eyes he descended the slope and walked away from The Old Mill. The future King James. That was his life and the love of his life was not part of it.

The Fairmile Green Man
By J.E. Hall

'As if this earth in fast thick pants were breathing' S T Coleridge

Is everything taken for granted? Are precious memories of our natural world, our beautiful Devon to be simply left to take a final gasp and die?

Today the river Tale quietly burbles and gurgles from its source in Devon's verdant Blackdown Hills before finally, little bigger than a stream, it reaches the river Otter which takes it in, embracing and enveloping it whilst murmuring more sonorous tones. Eventually, everything is swept into an expansive sea at Budleigh Salterton, where in a dark mingling all disappears, emptying into a vast horizon, the end of the Tale. But with climate change will all this be gone for ever?

But wait, return, go back, to the glinting and twisting Tale sparkling in the light over its short journey of 8.8 miles, the buzz of insects and singing of birds making accompanying music for those who hear it. As its clear water is borne ever south it feeds and nurtures the green banks, home to its lost and then returning water voles. Nearing the end of the stream's short course, between the settlements of Talaton and Ottery St Mary in East Devon, lies tiny Fairmile. This hamlet is remarkable only for the battle fought on its soil in the late 1990s, a vain attempt to save its precious copse of ancient oak trees. A generation on, was all they fought consigned to oblivion, does no memory remain?

Wind back to those years. It was here once upon a time the legendary eco-warrior Swampy and his fellow protesters gained national prominence for their green cause. When they lost, a new concrete causeway, the A30 by-pass was laid. This east-west 13 mile long dual carriageway, formed in haste across a no-mans-land, was laid upon the newly barren and denuded landscape. To the victor went the spoils. Human memories are short, politics are fickle and the battle for Fairmile now but a fading mythic folklore evocation from a by-gone generation, a far-distant ghostlike echo from the distant past. Occasionally in the pub at Whimple, a glass will be raised and the words, 'Cheers Swampy!' shared in remembrance.

However, with the passing years not everything is so easily destroyed as Fairmile's trees. Look inside the nearby ancient buildings which take the curious back a thousand years and more. Like sentinels they stand as guardians of deep truths. Inside the parish churches of Talaton and Ottery live signs and symbols in wood and stone from a pre-Christian age. These are the green men of old.

Numerous green men were subtly put in place by Medieval stone masons and wood carvers who, away from towny supervisors, formed these familiar reminders of nature and long-hidden gods to be eternal witnesses. They carefully shaped and brought to life their faces in wood and stone, tucking them away under seats, on high pillars and in lofty roof spaces. In their creation, nature was made magical, divinely precious and ordained, these watchers and keepers became tellers of a bigger story calling observers to 'play your part'. The many green men look down from on high, prompting, telling of an oft-forgotten dependent connectedness, men with trees and plants, in which all lives are hid. In nature's well-being the old gods were happy, but when forgetfulness rules all, nature's place at the heart of things, becomes perilous, desperate and desolate.

Recently discovered in the Lady Chapel, in St Mary's parish church, Ottery, are several more ancient green man ceiling bosses. They speak of Christian ambivalence as to their presence amongst the more overt Christian iconography, for one green man is inverted as if being denied a proper place. Though Christians have included the green man in their religious architecture, his presence raises more questions than answers. On the one hand, maybe, he reflects a degree of theological tolerance, a gentle inclusion of a far-distant pagan past and mysteries unknown. A time when God might be thought to speak through many means. On the other hand perhaps, like a Medieval doom painting, he warns of demons and false gods. Many green men are found across Devon. Not alone, they are connected with green man stories in Europe, the Middle and Far East. Gazing inscrutably with open mouths the world's numerous green men say what? Equally obscure, the meaning of the similar Woodwose carvings of wild men and women puzzles those who find them. The true meaning behind these rare, mystical, hairy woodland folk are likewise lost in time.

Today's A30, four lanes of unceasing, whooshing, elevated noise, made as the sound of metal, plastic and rubber thunder on, beats as if a victor's drum. This grey concrete surface is a giant reverberating gravestone. Fairmile's sacred space holds the burnt remains of its oaks buried deep. Every tyre overhead hammers down on oak ash beneath. Above ground, there's no written sign, no memorial seen to tell the Fairmile tale. Erased, obliterated is every green and living trace. This so-called 'improved' trunk road stands proud, built to serve the gods of 'more' and 'convenient' and 'fast' and 'profit', showing the latest divinities have moved in and made their brazen new home between Honiton and Exeter.

Spare a thought for those defenders who'd been watching through many lenses and first occupied the site in October 1994, those who'd fought long and hard in the field. Yes, they were a motley crew, sustained by green visions, dole money, pub visits and some recreational drugs. Their captain, Swampy with his subalterns, played cat and mouse, keeping contractors and their legal backers at bay. Throughout their campaign, a green army of eco-warriors headed up and below ground dodging their ever nearer adversaries making an easy target to throw condemning labels.

Mother earth received supportive tree top and underground communities, the growing protest site affectionately called 'Big Momma'. The popular word was that only one side could win this war of attrition, but the eco-warriors believed they were being the change they wanted to see. They absolutely believed the future depended on what they did.

Today, truth to tell, every last vestige of the nymet grove of green and rising trunk that once supported majestic canopies and singing birds has gone. Only a few vestigial, virtual images of what was, are to be found after scrolling searches deep in data streams in the iCloud. But on the ground only the ghosts of lost trees remain, perhaps seen dancing in the low clouds on misty, foggy, winter days in mystic shapes and forms. Towering above them all, like a huge heraldic flag on a bloody battlefield, stands silhouetted the mighty commanding shape of the giant oak reigning supreme. It holds out wide its strong majestic boughs, as if a mystic spectral tree built on steroids. Yet all is but a haunting of a once great wood.

Having stood there, an undisturbed, towering, watching Ent, ruling for hundreds of years, the giant was invaded and desecrated, a yellow jacket clad army of enemy running rampant over its host. They, like hungry wolves, were waiting for their chance to fall upon what would soon be but a dying carcass. They came with hungry urgency and in impatience hacked off its noble limbs one by one.

Noisy chainsaws, belching choking fumes proved unstoppable, the nails hammered in by defenders to halt their whirring blades proved no match for them. Lofty branches crashed down. Finally, its chunky disfigured torso was ripped from the ground by panting iron machinery, torn from the rich sandy soil which had mothered it from tiny acorn seed. Vast networks of underground communicating fibres that gave it sustenance and life sent their final messages of danger and death. Soon, upturned naked roots exposed to the air, were doused in carbon fossil fuel and torched to quickly burn in spluttering, spewing sap, bright red and savage orange flame. Swathes of dark grey suffocating smoke were seen by despondent and scattering watchers to be lifting clouds of ash high into the Devon sky, shutting out the winter sun.

The swirling, smoking cold skies told those who watched of a battle fought, won and lost. The victors cleared and scraped the land, bringing in foreign stones, adding deep layers of sterile foundation rock and smearing atop a dead and limey surface. To the anthem cries of 'more cars, vans and lorries' thirty pieces of silver in the form of thirty years of gross profits began to grease the palms of a distant American bank. The fortune spent on the eviction process soon forgotten as if small change. To capture the battle's end, the faces of bleary-eyed press photographers gathered like voyeurs round a never ending accident, eager to record in film and footage a story of inevitable and ultimate defeat.

It took more than two years for the above ground Allercombe site to be cleared, then on the 27th December 1996, the Fairmile site was lost too. Yet, even so, when all seemed lost, like human moles five warriors stayed underground with 'no surrender' their watchword. A cautious hard-hatted Under Sheriff of Devon, Trevor Coleman, paraded between giving interviews and instructing contractors. In desperation he brought in specialist cavers, increasingly fearful of tunnel collapse and human deaths on consciences.

Focussing down on 23 January 1997, the posse began chasing those remaining in their human wormery only to find steel doors blocking their way, then vertical hell-bound shafts and inadequate shoring; progress became dangerous, uncertain and slow.

Tory would-be councillor, Adrian Rogers went on TV to urge the law to do 'whatever it takes' and suggested filling the tunnels with gas. What did he have in mind, deadly cyanide, fumigation with Magnesium Phosphide or a little wood smoke? He never said. Meanwhile, as the fragile sandy burrows began to collapse, the five defenders – Swampy, John Woodhams, Muppet Dave, Animal and Ian, dug ever deeper. Using a US army tunnelling manual, they took their twisting warren down almost 50 feet into the Devon sand. Determined courage marked this stand.

In darkness the five ate their baked beans washed down with orange juice, telling their pursuers through the tannoy they'd starve rather than release themselves. Defiant words, yes, but maybe it's not that hard to tell yourself to starve on such a diet. Unsurprisingly in these subterranean catacombs, John became ill and gave himself up after a day. Then, after another five days of dig and chase in the dark there were three. Brave 'Animal', the sixteen year old Greta Thunberg of her day, emerged to say profoundly to the cameras, 'I'm glad I done what I come to do.' Ian too is pulled out. When asked why he did it, he replied simply, 'to defend the land.'

Only Muppet Dave and Swampy kept one step ahead in the ongoing dangerous game of ferrets and rabbits. By day seven Muppet Dave was caught, only Swampy alone remained with his book on Mahatma Ghandi for company. Ghandi's two central themes in his political teachings: satyagraha (the power of non-violence) and swaraji (self-rule and freedom) gave him solace and inspiration as he campaigned for nature's rightful place.

Within a week, on Thursday 30 January 1997, Swampy was caught; all was finally over. By then he was a national by-word, a peace protesting giant among men, a living legend. David Hooper from Berkshire had morphed into Swampy, becoming the Robin Hood of Fairmile against the big bad sheriff, the David against a mighty Goliath, the courageous little fellow who'd taken a stand for every little fellow who'd fought for his principles. Swampy was hauled before the waiting cameras, charged with obstruction by the police and told to appear later before no less a magistrate than David Cameron's mother.

With grossly indecent haste, driven by fear of more popular protest and that the giant oak would become, even in its remaining splintered shards a rallying point, a martyr's token, even a holy shrine, a desperate rallying effort was made by the contractors to remove its every trace.

Even so, at risk of apprehension and prosecution and by subterfuge and cunning, a sacred piece of the giant's oak soul, its heart wood, its strongest part, was stolen away from the razed and guarded site by an anonymous angel. Much later, at night, the same piece of precious timber was left with a message outside Henry Philip's door in nearby Alfington.

Henry knew wood and read its forms and textures, seeing its beckoning shapes and forms in 3D. Henry's gift was to bring wood to life with his craftsman's tools. In this heart wood piece of oak, Henry saw a grinning green man with jesting cheeks, piercing eyes and sprouting foliage escaping from his mouth. In his workshop his tools enlivened by the piece gave the ancient giant his human and divine face. Green and man became entwined, co-existing in mysterious co-dependence.

Look into the green man's eyes and it is as if his bright expression speaks. Look at his mouth and it is as if it moves in shapes and words, in a language we no longer understand. What is it he says?

These green men live in churches where worshippers and idle visitors gaze upon them. What do they see? Has a sermon ever mentioned them? If so was it to say that from dust we come and to dust we shall return, the green man as momento mori? Yet also is he not memento vitae showing the resurrection new life in green coming out of the dead skull's every orifice? A man of contradiction maybe? Or has, over time, Christ become the green man, the incarnate one, through whom all things were made? Maybe the green man has been christianised along with other aspects of the older pagan past.

Sometimes the flower ladies at their floral festivals recreate a bower of green and petalled wonder where the green man still feels at home. Christians both love and hate nature – it is fallen, unreliable, not to be trusted; yet is it also not the stuff of creation that sustains humankind, all made by God who feeds and waters it by his almighty hand?

Gandhi said, 'The earth, the air, the land and the water are not an inheritance from our forefathers but on loan from our children. So we have to handover to them at least as it was handed over to us.'

Looking back to the battle for Fairmile, the carved green man adorned by leaves of oak still tells his tale. Within a generation humankind and all natural life are being destroyed. The green man's smile turns to a mournful look as he watches on as mankind slowly lifts the air temperature, turning all that's green and alive, to fire and death. What's left of the River Tale's beauty either side of the A30 is again under threat. Nature cries.

Perhaps in Henry Philip's carved green man the heart of Fairmile's giant oak escaped total annihilation to offer us a timely warning.

Under the Hunters Moon
By K. Y. Eden

I crank open the window slightly to let in the icy air, cooling my tear strewn face. It's a relief to feel the biting wind as I speed up. The moor is quiet, not unusual for this time of year, and pleasing, as there are no dazzling car beams insight.

Yet, the Hunters Moon so bright, lights my path encouraging me, forwards, faster. I feel reckless, dangerous even, something I rarely experience any more, and for once I'm exhilarated. My car bounces on the dips in the uneven road and I do not care. Numb to all except speed. I'm not going anywhere, I'm anxious to get away. My humiliation still raw as the smug, righteous look on his mother's face silently lingers.

I turn on the radio and am greeted with a loud crackling noise, Exmoor offers a patchy signal for phone and radio. I swiftly switch to disc and flick through until I reach number eleven, the most obnoxious, loud track on the album. Anything to drown out my inner monologue of all the things I wish I said. And some that would probably make a sailor blush. The faster I drive the less I will care, the quicker I drive the greater the distance between me and him... and his whole sorry family.

Hot tears warm my wind stung cheeks as the road ahead blurs. I wipe the sodden mess which my face has become with the back of my hand. The car nipped the edge of the road pushing me across, I release a silent squeal as I try to recover control of the car as it increasingly vibrates up through the steering column. Panicking I brake, sending the car into a skid.

The moon momentarily hides behind a cloud and there — in the darkness, revealed only by my headlight was a huge horse galloping towards me. I scream and this time it is vocal. I pump the brake, the car spins and slides - within seconds the horse is over my bonnet. I close my eyes and feel the air bag deploy in my face.

I don't know how long has passed, it could be seconds, or minutes, or hours all I know is I'm cold. I begin to check my body, my feet move, my arms move, my head is sore but still mobile, although I can't hear anything, I strain harder to hear, but still nothing. Could this be a good thing? I hit an animal, surely it would be making a noise... unless I killed it.

The horror of that makes me sick, releasing the seat belt I barge the car door open, tumble out onto the frozen ground and vomit. Strangely the feel of the buckram frosted grass invites me to rest; I lie down and look at the illuminated path that the headlights carve. Relieved it was just me there, no-one to see me... broken. I blithely welcome sleep.

A deep voice beckons me to wake up, but I can't, my brain tells my eyes to open but they are sealed shut with ice and shame. 'Open your eyes' he tells me.

'I want to!' I reply, I hear him rustle and feel warmth spread over my body, a warmth that makes me ache and feel heavy, pushing me further into the earth. I feel him stroking my hair gently the way a parent does a weeping child, or a lover making hushed promises. It consoles me.

He leans closer to my ear and whispers, 'if you're not ready, I will stay with you until you are.' I smile to myself as I enjoy his heat and the tickle on my cheek every time he strokes my hair. All the pain felt distant, too distant to care about.

I lay there silently, still straining to comprehend every sound, I could make out the gentle movement of my companion and the faint sound of my heart beat... but that might be just for my ears to hear.

'It's time to wake up now' he says 'help is coming!'

'It is?' I croak, my eyelashes struggle to part as I see the slowly dimming beam of my headlight, 'Did you send for help?' I ask.

'Yes, I am always here for help, my Evelyn'

'My name's Lynne,' I say, thinking he must have misheard me, and wondering when I even told him my name. 'What's your name?' I whisper.

'It's William,' he replies.

'William, I like that name... Did you see me crash? I think I hit a horse... Oh God! What have I done?' my mind floods with memories. I try to sit up.

'Shush! Sit still, you're injured,' he commands.

'Okay!' I reply pulling myself closer and resting my head on his soft fur coat, it smelt sweet... sweet William. 'How did you find me? Why are you here on the moor so late?' I ask, I realise I should just be grateful he is, but curiosity gets the better of me.

'Well... Lynne, I always cross the moor this time at night, my home is just over there and every evening I check the herd.' I can't see where he is pointing but it's soothing just to listen to him. He talks for ages about the farms surrounding Exmoor, the people who live there, who is good and who is best to keep away from. He speaks fondly of the animals that graze the land, as if he knows them all by name. I feel safe, comforted, until he gently places my head that rests contently on him, back on the harsh unforgiving ground.

'Wait! Where are you going?' I squeak. 'Don't go — please don't leave me!' I feel panic rise up through my chest.

'Look up!' he says gently. I follow his eyeline and see a helicopter search light sweep the ground. Enough light trickles into our path sufficient for me to make out his outline, he is huge, majestic. I try to speak, to beg him to stay but the searchlight blinds me. I close my eyes and he is gone.

The sound of the helicopter fills my ears. Evoking tears of relief and sadness in duality. 'William', I call out, above the droning of the helicopter, 'William... William please!' I feel dizzy and sick again as I close my eyes once more. The cold envelops me and I long for my companions warmth.

I hear a distant voice 'Miss, Miss... grab the stretcher Joe, and bring another blanket,' a woman's voice, light and airy fills my ears. 'It's okay Miss, my name is Lucy, I'm a medic with the Air Ambulance, what's your name?' I cannot answer. 'No matter,' she says clearing her throat, 'we are going to take you to hospital in the helicopter... don't worry it's quite good fun, isn't it Joe?' I didn't hear Joe answer but felt another person move my feet. 'It won't be long now we just need to strap you in nice and secure,' she continues whispering in part to Joe as they tighten the straps around my body making it impossible for me to move.

I watch Lucy clip the radio back into her belt, she catches my eye and smiles, moving closer she says, 'Okay Lynne, is it? We will be moving you any minute now, you will soon warm up. Is there anyone you want me to contact for you?' I thought for a moment, not any longer, I was alone... again. 'Anyone at all?' she asks once more.

'William,' I said faintly, 'Sweet William.'
'Okay, William who? Is he a relative?' Lucy asks as she takes the other end of the stretcher and shuffles towards the helicopter.

'No, er! I don't know!' I feel panicky again, 'he was here with me just before you arrived, he lives over there somewhere on the moor.'

Lucy stops, taking Joe by surprise and looks around 'I didn't see anyone else here, did you Joe?'

'Nope I've not seen anyone up here... not until we found you!' he says, sliding the stretcher into the helicopter.

'But he was with me, he told me he got help, and what about the horse I hit?' I try to move but can only lift my head a few inches.

'Someone from the farmhouse at the edge of the village called it in, they saw strangely angled headlights on for an unusually long time. No one could get through to check it out. Search and Rescue teams have been trying to reach you most of the night... Well – we got you now and the rest doesn't matter, you rest, we will get all the answers tomorrow,' she says reassuringly.

The whirring noise and the motion of the helicopter makes me drowsy, I am desperate to remember the things William told me. I try to call for him but peace finally crashes in at my final blink.

William circles my thoughts, I remember little else as I gaze up at the stark white lights of the hospital side room, I am painless. My mind clear and the foggy memories of the preceding day are lifted. A nurse, with her back to me is sorting through my blooded clothes on the stand under the tiny barred window. I look down to see I have been cleaned up and put in an unattractive hospital gown. I watch the nurse for a few moments and ask if anyone had been in to see me, she doesn't answer, maybe she didn't catch what I said. I clear my throat and say, more loudly this time, 'did you find William? I want to thank him you see, he was so sweet and stayed with me until the helicopter came,' I try to sound upbeat.

This time she turns and looks at me, her soft aged face sad as she says, 'now young lady, let's smarten you up a bit,' she combs my hair away from my face, just as gently as William had, and hums a pretty tune that I do not recognise. Placing the comb down she says, 'Right my lovely, I'm going to take these tubes out now, you don't need them any longer.' She is so gentle, I try to lift my arm to make it easy for her but she has it under control, I watch her face as she lightly takes out the tubes.

Another nurse enters carrying hospital linen, I smile at her, she is significantly younger but just as gracious.

'Well? How did you get on Katie?' the older nurse asks the younger one.

'Not too well; to be honest,' Katie replies solemnly, 'I can't find any close relatives at the moment, only an ex-boyfriend who won't even take my calls!' - *Ha! I know how that feels, poor girl* - The troubled young nurse rubs her forehead and continues to say, 'I spoke to the team, they said that she was talking about her having someone with her before they got there, but we reckon it must have been the brain injury to make her think that.' The two nurses exchange a gloomy look as they unwrap the starchy sheet Katie bought in with her.

'Did she say who she thought was with her?' the older nurse asks, she pauses and looks intensely at Katie.

'Yes! She said he was called William.' Katie shrugs and continues - 'Oh yes! And she said something about hitting a horse... but the rescue team said they didn't see any injured animals up there.'

I want to speak, I know they are talking about my William, but I can't get the words out. I feel the world stop, I sense every particle, every colour, every minute detail rich in existence, and slowly, organically, in slow motion the world moves again to its natural rhythm.

I watch the older nurses face as she silently arrives at a decision. She faintly smiles, pats my arm and says, 'sweet William, bittersweet William, the ghost horse of Exmoor, he always takes a soul at the fullest Hunters Moon... and now sadly, he has another for his herd...'

Katy pulls the crisp white linen sheet over my head, as the older nurse ceremonially opens the tiny barred window and says, 'now your spirit is free.'

Make a Wish
By Richard Dee

It was another warm summer's evening in Devon. Outside *The Prince William*, on Brixham harbour, people were sitting around large wooden tables, eating, drinking and watching the sunset. The sun sank through a cloudless sky, reflecting in shades of orange across the waters of Torbay, bathing the moored yachts and the crowds in its amber glow.

Steve Pengelly had organised a birthday party for his wife and family, there were about thirty of their friends and family present. They had pulled tables together to make one large one.

Steve was tired, as a police detective, he was used to long hours. By his reckoning, he had been awake for a little over thirty, his body craved sleep. He couldn't miss tonight though, Lyn would give him more grief than his superintendent. It had taken him ages to select a date when everyone could come down, they had eaten delicious local seafood and were now settled into that easy, relaxed part of the evening where the drink flowed and everyone was happy and mellow.

'Alright, love?' Lyn asked, turning away from her brother and placing her hand on his arm. The sixth sense that all married couples shared told her how tired he was, she hoped that he understood how much this evening had meant to her. 'Thanks for arranging this, I know you've been really busy lately and it means a lot.'

Steve smiled, 'I'm glad you're enjoying it, sorry I'm a bit tired, long day.'

'And the night before,' she said, concern in her voice, 'I'm used to it.' He worked too hard, they were all busy nights lately, reduced manning and increasing crime was as much a problem here as it was in the city. They had come here to get away, have a better life, it had been until recently. Steve was a good man and a good husband and father. He took it seriously, catching bad men, she knew that he saw a lot of things that affected him and she tried to be supportive. He deserved more time to enjoy the place. 'Day off tomorrow?'

Steve laughed and took a drink of his beer. 'I wish, I might get away with a ten o'clock start but I've got paperwork coming out of my ears.'

Before she could answer, there was a sudden lightening of the sky, everyone stopped talking and looked up.

A shooting star flashed above them, a blazing white streak of fire. As it passed overhead, the sound caught up with it, a low rumbling echoed across the bay. A black line of what looked like smoke lingered behind, marking its passage.

'That's big,' muttered Lyn.

'And close,' added her brother Terry, a local fisherman. 'Looks like it'll land in the sea, just off Thatcher Rock.'

'Make a wish,' said Lyn, as it disappeared behind the hills of Torquay.

Steve could think of several, a good night's sleep was top of his list, followed by another detective to help him out. Finally, he settled for a night without a call to go and sort out someone else's problems.

~ ~ ~ ~

Tim and Sylvia always walked Skipper, the Labrador in the morning, just after the beach café opened, so that they could have coffee and chat to the other dog walkers; before the crowds arrived on Oddicombe beach. It was only ten minutes' walk from their bungalow, a bit of a trek back up the hill afterwards but worth it for the views, the exercise a good excuse for a cake to go with their coffee.

The talk among the walkers who they saw every day was of the shooting star, two days ago. Maud had been taking her spaniel for a last stroll and had seen it pass almost directly overhead, before plunging into the sea, about three miles offshore. Yesterday, she had explained it all to anyone who would listen, waving her arms to indicate the motion, beside her, the spaniel slept, hair matted from his swim. 'I was in the Herald,' she said, 'they reckoned that the T.V. people might turn up to interview me but nothing happened.'

They were earlier today, the café was still closed. Skipper was getting old and rarely ran, although he loved a swim. As they passed the café, they came to an area where rocks had fallen and blocked the end of the beach. Instead of turning, Skipper suddenly set off, barking loudly. 'What's got into him?' wondered Tim. 'Goodness knows,' replied Sylvia, 'I just hope it's not another dead fish.'

Skipper had found a part decomposed mackerel on the beach, he would not relinquish it, it had made him stink for weeks afterwards, no matter what they did. They followed him and saw that he had spotted a dark shape, in among the rocks, just above the high tide line.

Skipper was poking at the shape with his snout, turning to bark urgently as the two hurried along.

'It's a man,' said Sylvia, 'come here, Skipper.'

The man was laying head down on the pebbles. Dressed in nothing but a pair of blue shorts, his back was covered in fine blonde hair, crisscrossed by small scars. Sylvia knelt by his side, felt for a pulse on one outstretched wrist.

'He's alive,' she said, 'he has a strong pulse.' She shifted her position, felt for his head.

'Don't move him,' suggested Tim, 'he might have a broken neck.'

'I'm just checking his airway,' she replied, 'there's quite a bit of bruising, but it's already fading. Goodness knows how long he's been here. Make yourself useful, Tim. Take Skipper away. See if the café's open, call an ambulance.'

~ ~ ~ ~

Torbay hospital's Accident and Emergency department were used to receiving bodies pulled from the sea, fishermen, over-enthusiastic holidaymakers and drunk students convinced they were Olympic swimmers were run of the mill, so when the blonde man arrived it raised barely a ripple. Anyway, this one was breathing, had no obvious broken bones or internal trauma so wasn't a priority.

He was unconscious, which scored him a few points and unidentified, which got him a few more, and a bed in a single room. He was subjected to a barrage of tests, blood was drawn for analysis. Half-way through the procedures, he woke. When asked his name, he got agitated, said that he couldn't remember. He was restrained, the police were informed.

Steve Pengelly took the call. It was a welcome diversion from his paperwork, he set off with a constable in tow.

On arrival, he introduced himself. He was relieved to see a face he knew in the chaos that was A and E, even this early in the day. Trish, the sister on duty knew him well enough. They had shared enough night shifts, him trying to question suspects and victims, her trying to heal them.

'Hi Trish,' said Pengelly, 'I've come to see the boy from the beach.'

'He's in four,' she said, 'still a bit groggy but everything checks out. No broken bones, no internal injuries. He's been lucky, as far as we can tell it's just cuts and bruises. He can't remember anything though. He panicked when he couldn't tell us his name, tried to leave. We had to restrain him.'

'Concussion?'

'Maybe,' she said, nodding. 'His brain function seems OK, no bleeds on the scan, it'll all come back to him in the end.'

'Any identification?' Steve was still hoping for an easy job.

'Nothing, just a pair of shorts, no shoes, no phone or wallet.'

'Anything from the scene?'

'I don't think there was much. Dog walkers found him, two of them have come in with him. They're in the café, I told them to hang around for you.'

Pengelly thanked her and dispatched the constable to find them and arrange to get statements. 'Let's go and say hello,' he suggested.

'Did you see the shooting star?' she asked as they walked towards room four.

'I did,' he replied, 'it made a cheap fireworks display for Lyn's birthday.'

She laughed, 'the papers said it was unusual to get that close. They normally burn up well before they reach the ground.'

'It would have made a mess of Torbay,' he said, 'at least it landed in the sea.'

When they entered the room, Pengelly could see that the boy was calm. Good, he thought, that would make his job a lot easier. The mystery man was lying on his back, blue eyes gazing at the ceiling. Straps held his hands and feet, one crossed his stomach. A drip was fitted in his left arm, 'saline, he might be dehydrated,' explained Trish, 'we don't know how long since he ate or drank last. It could be affecting his memory.'

'Hello sir,' Pengelly said softly, 'I'm detective Pengelly, can you hear me?'

'Yes,' replied the man, 'Where am I?' His voice was soft; hesitant, as if he was searching for the right words.

'You're in Torbay hospital A and E,' Trish replied, 'we found you on the shore at Oddicombe beach.'

'I don't know where that is,' said the man.

'Do you know your name, your address?' asked Pengelly. 'Is there anyone who we can contact, a wife, parent? Don't be alarmed, you're not in any trouble, we just want to know who you are, get you fit and home safe.'

The man shook his head, 'my name is... John,' he said it with difficulty; as if dredging it up from the depths of his mind. 'The rest, I don't know.' His tone suggested desperation, the sudden realisation that he could remember nothing. He rattled the straps, 'what's happened to me, why am I held down?'

'You tried to leave, it's for your own safety,' said Trish.

'What's the last thing you remember?' asked Pengelly.

'Falling,' he replied; almost instantly, 'then water all around me.' He struggled to rise, pulling against the straps. 'I have to get back, tell them what's happened, they'll be waiting, they need to know.'

'Who? Tell me and I can tell them.'

He fell back, 'I can't...'

Trish stopped Pengelly at that point, 'that's enough Steve, let him rest, his memory will come back, just give him time.'

She hustled him away, 'we'll call you if anything changes, he'll be moved up to a medical ward later today. There'll probably be an assessment by the psychs before we decide what to do.'

'Thanks, Trish, I'll go and track my constable down, get a statement from the witnesses. See you later.' As he walked away, he considered all the possible ways of finding out this man's identity. So much for an easy job.

~ ~ ~ ~

Jahan relaxed, his initial fear and sense of helplessness slowly replaced by calm and confidence. The bipeds hadn't seen through his disguise. The abductions had all been worth it, the careful gathering of bodies had enabled scientists to create their own version of the human form, install him inside it. It appeared to have been successful, none of the primitive medical equipment had detected his true nature.

The memory in the host brain was filled with information on this world, the nanites had done a sterling job of repairs to his body and bones since his involuntary soaking. All his systems were nearly back to full operation. He knew he could snap his bonds easily, his muscles were more than capable. But he had decided that it would not help him to do so.

He had bigger problems, his ship was gone, lost in the liquid water that abounded on this world, the reason for his mission. He had no way of telling his people that he lived, he would have to wait for another to come, somehow alert them to his presence and hope for rescue. He knew that his mate on Theth and his offspring would grieve for him, he felt sorrow for their suffering.

If he had to stay in this place they called Torbay, he would have to adapt, quickly. He needed to find a biped to assist him. They could never know his true purpose, as the advance guard of a conquering race. He could use his pretence of memory loss to ensnare them, make them help him.

There was still plenty of information about the planet and its defences that the high council needed, information that he could gather and store, ready to present when the time came. If he searched hard enough, he might be able to fashion a means of communication, to let them know he was alive and still working for the cause. He thought of the bipeds he had seen so far, evaluated their usefulness, suitability.

There was Trish, the old woman in the uniform. He dismissed her, he could see that she was suffering from a tumour, she would expire soon, he might have many of their years to wait. The detective? No, he would grow suspicious; anyway, he was of an age that would probably already have a mate, being the same gender as he, friendship might not be acceptable. That would be another thing he must be wary of.

The door opened again, he noticed a new scent in the room, some sort of flower overlaid the pheromones of a female.

'Hello John,' she called; it was the sound of a young voice. He noticed with interest that some of his shell's functions had changed, the pressure of the blood flow increased, he felt his outer skin warming. The eyes seemed to take in more light, lung capacity increased by a little over..., eight per cent.

'How are you feeling now?' She continued, making a clanking noise as she moved some hidden equipment. Jahan turned his head, she had her back to him, bending over to reach something. The part of his brain that had been constructed from human experiences told him that the bipeds regarded the view as pleasant.

'The doctor says that you're not from around here,' she continued, 'how do you like Devon?'

What was this effect, why did she make his body behave in this way? It was only a construction of DNA and manufactured flesh, grown in a laboratory. All the human functions and memories were controlled by a processor chip in the head. It was only supposed to cover his frame and change its appearance, making him acceptable to the bipeds. There was no intention to make it independently sentient, yet by some means, its nucleic acid was doing just that. He sensed an attraction for her, how had this body taken on emotion? It seemed to register parts of the consciousness of the humans, the ones who had been harvested to make it?

'It's very nice,' he said, 'I've never been in a place like this before.' That, at least, was true.

'You should stay,' she suggested, 'I can help you find somewhere; until you get your memory back.'

As if I have a choice, he thought.

~ ~ ~ ~

She stood up, turned and he saw her face for the first time. It was a different face to everyone else's, oval, tanned, surrounded by short hair and huge brown eyes. And her shell, it was more curved than his, more than the older female's had been. It too was pleasant. He noted that her face was flushed. Her body seemed to be exhibiting the same changes as his. She must feel the attraction too. He felt his mouth move into a smile.

'Did you see the shooting star?' she asked. 'Two nights ago, it was amazing.'

'No,' replied Jahan, 'I did not.' He was unwilling to tell her that it wasn't a star, it was his ship, out of control and crashing into the sea.

'Oh well, never mind, there'll be others, my grandmother tells me, if you see one, you should make a wish.'

Jahan pulled the relevant memory from the brain in his shell, understood the concept instantly. The nanites must have completed their repairs, his recall was now fully restored. Almost without realising it, he wished for his people to come and save him, take him back to his mate. Even while he thought it, he knew that wishful thinking would get him nowhere. He had to come up with another plan. Perhaps he could use the mutual attraction to his advantage. In return, as he was here, he could try to make her existence happy.

Then he wondered, why was he behaving like this, the shell was clearly affected by the female's presence, could it be influencing him? Should he feel such guilt, thinking of this biped in that way?

Was he not Jahan, here as a conqueror, to take everything that he could from these primitives? Yet he was suddenly full of doubt. It was almost disloyal; he was happily mated, with cubs of his own. But that was on Theth, light years distant. Was it just self-preservation that made him realise, he was here, he had to blend in. Who knew when he would sit under the blood red sun of his home world again?

She must have taken his silence for doubt. 'Would you like me to help you, mysterious John?' she said. 'Just until your memory returns; or your family arrive.'

Jahan was aware that she was about the same age as he was designed to appear. She had many years ahead of her. They could grow old together. Perhaps a wait on this planet; in this Devon, might not be such a bad thing after all.

'I think that would be good,' he replied.

What's in a name? Church Chatter
By Jenifer Braund

'Me an' the others got together because of Angela and Joy. Well 'twas the Vicar really I suppose; you see 'e 'ad this three year mission idea, trying to shake us all up a bit, 'an he wuz new; well 'e only came four years ago and that's new 'ere abouts. Anyways one afternoon a week they 'as bible study; you know the sort of thing, 'avin' a look at next week's readings an' thinking 'bout what they means here and now for us volks. Well 'twas a bit diff'rent when they was writ wadn't it. All them different peoples and them suppressed by them Romans, and 'avin' to pay taxes to 'em an all. Come to think of it p'rhaps it wadn't so diff'rent!

Aggie Mason she said she'd 'ave a go at that group, her man's a builder, nice bloke always 'elpful; she started it with Lizzie Motheringham; yeah funny name in'it, 'er being the local midwife an' all? I went along fer a bit, but I does me flowers I likes a bit of peace an' quiet, that's why I joined Angie's group. They does this silent prayer stuff. ' Contemplation', Vicar calls it. They says a bit from the bible, or from one of them Holy books, or a bit of poetry; I likes that best, I likes a bit of poetry I do, then you closes yer eyes an' just thinks about it, a verse or just a word. You let's ev'rything else go, all the worries and chores an' stuff for twenty or thirty minutes. Then we sez the Grace and 'as a nice chat over a cuppa. Not much more than an hour but it's amazin' 'ow much better you feels after. The Vicar, he says that God talks to us in the silence, an' we can't hear Him speak if we're thinking this and that all the time.

There's another funny thing, Joyce he's called. No not 'is first name 'is second, he's the Reverend Richard E Joyce. Can't recall that he's ever said what 'is middle name is, but when you see it writ down you'll see what I mean. REJoyce rejoice see? Then there's my friend 'ilda, she's married to Bert Baker, you'll never believe it, 'e's the village baker. Angie's not married, but you know 'ow it is these days, you'm either married, single, divorced or livin' in sin. That's what my Reg says. Our Billie gives 'im a look, goes on about being politically correct, clever our Billie, should 'ave gone to university last year but when Reg was took sick, stayed to help out, liked it and stayed on. Like the Vicar says it's a good business and good to keep it in the family. Mind you it was my mother-in-law insisted in putting in the apostrophe and making the name sound posh. Reginald De'ath Funeral Directors!

Reg says undertakers was good enough for Granddad and Uncle Bill, but there you are she always had airs and graces that one. Comes of marrying beneath 'erself that's what Bessie Appleyard says. Her family still 'as the cider orchards and makes the best scrumpy here abouts my Reg says. I likes a sweeter drop of cider meself. Still always makes for a good 'arvest lunch 'cos her Dan always sends down a barrel of his best.

Anyway I was tellin' you about Angie's quiet group wadn't I? There's a dozen of us now, 'tis amazin' how popular it's become our weekly bit o' silence. Joy Bell, she's a teacher at the village school, 'an she says it 'adn't 'alf calmed the children down. After school dinner when they all bin getting' excited in the playground, she settles 'em down with a bit of quiet music then silence. Started with five minutes an' now it's fifteen. 'An my goodness what a difference she says. Reading, 'rithmatic, 'istory, all the marks 'ave gone up, they kids aren't 'alf improved. So just goes to show dunnit. An' Angie she's now doing it with the pre-school littl'uns. When the tinies 'ave their naps the 3-4 year old 'ave there bit of quiet, so what about that then? The vicar when he drops in then, 'e calls it 'Place of Angels'. Angie's pre-school that is, 'er names Angela Place you see.

Now ain't that funny, you go down our street and nearly all of us is named after our trade. I tell you the signs says it all.

Mason's the builder; Bert the baker; Appleyards the cider works;

Now let's see you can't really count Joy, though it is Belltown Primary! The old foundry 'as long gone but they used to cast bells and whatnot before the war. I nearly forgot, Annie Lambs the farm shop, beautiful bit o' lamb they 'as there, properly hung too. Before they closed the post office, the old Misses Stampe ran all their lives, and their father before 'em. I'm sure 'twas the closure that finished Flo off, and Jessie none to good either. But like my Reg says, it's all good business one way or another, for 'im and Reverend Joyce anyhow. I nearly forgot, where they put up them rural offices, down t'other end of village, beyond Billie Carrs taxi service down at Lane End garage, we got Wills and Wills, solicitors; and Payless the accountants, but none of us believe that, does us?'

Twyford After Midnight
By Brian Willis

There is a town named Twyford in the West of England.

It is a place avoided at all costs once the midnight hour is struck.

No locals are to be found on the streets,

Even the feral children that plague the centre of town

would be home at whatever hovels they sprang from.

Rough sleepers are a rarity,

Unless so stupefied alcohol or drugs that nothing touches them.

For as midnight strikes,

The Shape Shifters come.

First they appear as opaque shadows,

then formulated into something more tangible.

Any unfortunate person observing this occurrence would be struck dumb with terror at what they beheld.

For whatever dark imaginings that lurked in the depths of their subconscious minds would be brought to the surface and projected back to them in terrifying images created by the Shape Shifters.

They would then lose all reason and become a gibbering imbecile.

For the unwary traveler, Twyford is off the beaten track.

Situated as it is in the North Devon triangle, that is made up of the M 5 motorway, the North Devon Link Road and the Tarka rail line that runs from Exeter to Barnstaple.

It is backwater that is seldom visited.

Twyford Police Station does a special patrol at ten minutes past four am. every morning.

For some mystic reason, the Shape Shifters, at four am, fade into the ether.

A special unmarked Police van, with a padded compartment in the back, sets out from the rear yard of the Police Station, to do its morning patrol.

If it comes across a gibbering victim of the Shape Shifter's curse, the said victim would then be deposited in the back of the padded van.

The victim would be taken to Arkham asylum on the edge of town, incarcerated for life.

Their reason would never return.

So my friend, if you're travelling the byways of North Devon and you see a sign post for Twyford, don't be tempted to take that road.

Turn around and drive swiftly in the opposite direction.

The Jeremy Thorpe affair: a baptism of fire, car windows & hub caps!! By Richard Lappas

This tale of intrigue, plotting in smoke-filled rooms and conspiracy to murder, that dominated the news agenda for close on a decade, ended with a courtroom full of chaos at the Old Bailey in London. The story unfolded in two areas of the country, one in London where Jeremy Thorpe resided as leader of the Liberals and the other in Devon where he lived in his beloved constituency of North Devon.

The scandal arose out of allegations from male model Norman Scott that he had been in a homosexual relationship with Thorpe at a time when such acts were illegal. Scott persisted with his allegations when Thorpe was leading a resurgent Liberal party. Attempts to silence him were unsuccessful until a hired gunman shot Scott's dog Rinka and that brought the affair out into the open. A subsequent trial involved Thorpe and three others being tried for conspiracy to murder Scott, but all were acquitted.

The highlight however for this novice working photographer was the vast number of car shots that I failed to achieve in the 8 weeks I spent covering the remands in the very cold seaside resort of Minehead in West Somerset. Reporting restrictions had been lifted on day one of the hearing; that meant that the whole story would come out straight away.

Every defendant and every star witness arrived at court, left for lunch, returned after lunch and then departed at the end of the day, hidden under a blanket in a car! My films were going back by dispatch rider twice a day and every day there was silence from the office in Exeter. With no pagers or mobile phones, this meant hours and hours of waiting, not knowing if I'd got the picture of the day or in fact if I had got no picture at all!

In the end, it became a car window too far as, night after night, the stars of the day were either driven or roared out of the court house which for a novice like me, gave little hope of getting at even a face in the picture but instead I achieved an amazing collection of car windows and hub caps!!! With fierce competition (all the national boys were in town), it was a high pressure job which was stretching me to the limit and beyond but as time went on, the pictures got better and I could almost hear the smiles back in Exeter!

The story concluded at the Old Bailey where the four defendants were found not guilty. The story had involved car chases, late night door knocks, door steps, Norman Scott playing football on Dartmoor etc. Such was the regularity of staff journalists doing watches every weekend at Jeremy Thorpe's home in the village of Cobbaton, that a 5 a side football league was formed and we used the car park of the Imperial hotel in Barnstaple as the pitch!

One of my early shots of Jeremy showed him in his best light, out on the hustings, talking to the people about every day issues and pushing the message that he so emphatically believed in as leader of his party.

For me, as a working photographer, Jeremy Thorpe was a godsend. He knew how to make it work for the press, he made pictures out of nothing at all. If he was visiting a farmer, he wouldn't just walk in, he'd be over the five-bar gate first and then do the talking. For us, he was a class act and would go out of his way to help, although even I have to admit to getting a bit fed up taking pictures of Jeremy Thorpe trying to feed Peter the duck in his back garden!

Maybe it's best summed up by my FaceBook posting on hearing of his passing:

'A sad day for many old friends in the Liberal Party with the passing of former party leader Jeremy Thorpe who has passed away....he was a lovely guy to deal with, always helpful and made great pictures ..something today's clueless clowns in the Commons should take note of. RIP Jeremy. Rich L'

Guardians
by Tracey Norman

It all started with that damned pond. How I wish we had never decided to go ahead with it.

At first, the idea sounded wonderful. Our new house in Devon was built in the seventies and had a huge back garden, which had apparently once been part of the nearby woods. It was mostly lawn, with a few flower beds here and there and a couple of vegetable patches. There was a flat area at the far end, shaded by trees, which Chris had fallen in love with because it reminded him of Monet's garden. I'd never been there, so I couldn't see it as he did. To me, it was just a slightly dark, boring area where things didn't grow very well. A pond would transform it.

We had been living in the house for about a year at that point and I still awoke most mornings feeling like the luckiest person alive. When we first moved in, I'd asked around to see if anyone had any anecdotes about the house, but only Trevor Smith had volunteered anything. Trevor was the local drunk, however, with a special line in tall tales. He was sitting at the end of the bar, leaning forward so far that his head was almost touching it. He was so still that I thought he was asleep, but as I waited for Stella, the landlady, to refill my glass, he looked over at me with bloodshot eyes. He lifted his glass and downed the contents in one long, practiced swallow. 'Lot of 'istory in that 'ouse,' he mumbled.

'Really?' I perked up, curious. 'What sort of history? We were told the house was only built in the seventies.'

'Goes back longer'n that,' he said, gesturing with his empty glass.

Trevor launched into a long, rambling explanation, most of which was so slurred that I could hardly understand him. 'Bloody mist' was clear enough, as was 'darkness', but none of it made any sense. At one point, he started talking about someone riding a horse across Exmoor. As I handed Stella my money, she caught my eye and shook her head, flicking her gaze over to Trevor. I nodded and gave a little shrug. After about twenty minutes, Trevor lapsed into a brooding silence. I thanked him, bought him a pint and went to sit at the other end of the bar.

I had added a few plants to the flower beds over the months, but other than that, we'd just maintained what was already there. Once the house was sorted, we started thinking about the garden. Chris suggested a pond.

A few sketches and a chat at the local garden centre later, Chris began digging. He had decided to make the pond around four feet deep – enough for a few koi carp – and about ten feet in diameter, so it was going to take several days.

After Chris had got rid of the sparse turf, I grabbed a spade and started helping him to dig. I thought I was doing a pretty good job until Chris said, 'Sophie, what on earth are you doing?'

I looked round. 'Digging?'

He smiled. 'Not your thing, is it?'

I gave an indignant huff. 'I've dug a hole,' I retorted, swinging my spade round so I could gesture with it. Unfortunately, the handle was a bit longer than I realised and Chris had to leap out of the way to avoid being kneecapped.

'Blimey, watch it,' he protested. 'Why not stick the blade straight into the ground and put a bit of weight on it? You might find that easier.'

I eye-rolled internally. Chris didn't often mansplain, but he had his moments. I dutifully followed his instructions, jabbing the spade into the soil with all my strength. I glanced over at Chris, who had opened his mouth to say something else. Catching my eye, he changed his mind and turned back to his own work. My spade hadn't gone very far into the ground, so I stood on the blade and jumped on it. The blade didn't budge, so I tried again, putting my whole weight into it. I overbalanced, fell off, crashed into Chris and we both sprawled onto the ground.

As we got back to our feet, Chris took my spade and laid it to one side. 'Tell you what,' he said, 'why don't you go and put the kettle on while I do a bit more out here?'

'I'm fine to carry on,' I reassured him, reaching for the spade, but he pushed it further away.

'I'd love a coffee,' he said pointedly. I blinked at him for a moment, then sloped off back to the house. It was probably safer that way. For both of us.

Looking back, it was around then that strange things began happening, although neither of us realised at the time. It was stupid, everyday things at first.

'Soph!' Chris called from the hallway. 'Have you seen my car keys?'

'They're on the hall table, love,' I called back from the bedroom, where I was wrestling with the duvet cover.

'No, they aren't.'

I rolled my eyes. Chris was wonderful and I loved him dearly, but sometimes it was like living with a child. I scowled at the duvet, dumped it onto the mattress and went downstairs. 'They're in the key tray, Chris. You always put them in the ... oh.'

He gave me one of his 'I told you so' looks, which never failed to irk me. Together, we hunted for the stupid keys for almost half an hour, before I discovered them in one of Chris's walking boots in the hall cupboard. I stood staring at them, confused, before remembering that he had been wearing those boots earlier and had dumped everything haphazardly in the hall before shooting upstairs for a shower. He must have knocked the keys off the table without realising.

I teased him for a while, then we both forgot about it. We also forgot about the number of times my pens went missing over the next few days, how two of the plant pots on the kitchen windowsill had been swapped over and why one of my favourite shirts simply vanished – although that one did, in fairness, take a lot longer to dismiss than everything else. There was a whole host of other odd but insignificant things that we didn't pay much attention to, beyond being amazed that we couldn't recall where we were leaving things. I actually joked to Chris one day that I was considering having myself tested for early-onset Alzheimer's because my memory was getting so bad. He didn't reply and when I glanced over, he was frowning.

'I don't think there's anything wrong with you,' he said. 'There's been a lot of strange stuff going on lately.'

'In what way strange?' But even as I said it, I felt goosebumps rise on my arms and I gave an involuntary shudder.

'Things disappearing from one place and turning up in another,' said Chris. 'Please tell me that it's not just my imagination. Your shirt – the blue one – did that ever turn up?'

'No,' I said slowly. 'You're right. Things have been a bit weird. I thought at first that it was you winding me up.'

'I thought you were winding *me* up!'

'So what is it, then?' I wondered aloud, but neither of us had an answer.

The discussion continued into the following day, when we were planning to go and pick up the pond lining. I spent the morning hunting around the end of the garden for any sizeable rocks that we could use to weigh the lining down, while Chris sat next to the pond with a tape measure, scribbling in a notebook. Every now and then, I thought I heard a voice whispering, but whenever I paused to listen, it stopped. At first, I didn't think much of it, but after a while, it became disconcerting.

'Where is that whispering sound coming from?' I asked.

Chris looked up from his notebook and listened for a few moments. A frown creased his brow and he shrugged. 'I can't hear any whispering,' he said. 'It's probably the trees or something.' He went back to his calculations and I stared at his profile while the whispers rose to a crescendo around me before abruptly dying away. Why couldn't he hear it? What on earth was going on?

A gentle serenity returned to the garden, but I could feel goosebumps along the length of my arms and I shivered, even though it was a warm day. Oblivious, Chris frowned at his notebook, chewing the end of the pencil, then announced that he was ready to go. I was so relieved to get away that I almost ran to the car.

The trip to the garden centre was uneventful and we arrived home with what I considered an excessive amount of pond lining. I'd asked Chris at the till if it wasn't too much, which hadn't gone down too well. By the time we got home, he was getting rather tetchy about it, so I dropped the subject and helped him lug the stuff through the garage and down to the pond.

We laid the lining out and started moving it into place. It was incredibly cumbersome and both of us were soon ready for a coffee. 'Let's just get this bit done,' Chris suggested, 'then I'll make a drink. Can you pull that corner over a bit towards the middle?'

I grabbed the section he indicated and tugged at it while he guided it from the edge of the pond. It was heavy and I needed a little more leverage, so I dug my heels in and leaned back, putting all my weight into it. All that happened was my hot hands lost their grip and I landed flat on my back. Chris snorted with laughter, then jumped down beside me to help me up. I caught his hand and was about to push myself to my feet when my knuckle hit something cold and lumpy just beside me and made me look down to see what it was.

I thought at first that it was a stone, but when I looked more closely, I realised it was the edge of something metal. I prodded at it.

'We'd better dig this out,' I said. 'It might tear the lining. It's quite rough.'

Chris went off to get a trowel and excavated around the object, which turned out to be long and thin with a slightly bulbous end. He dug down just enough that he could wrap one hand around it, then carefully worked it free.

I caught my breath. 'Wow, that looks lethal.'

Chris turned the object over in his hands. 'It looks like a bloody great nail,' he said.

'Well, at least it won't be ripping a bloody great hole in the pond lining,' I remarked, using the trowel to fill in the hole and smoothing the earth as best I could. 'Chuck it over there with those stones and the stuff for the tip.'

He turned and slung the metal object onto the pile. It landed with a loud clang that made me start, even though I was watching. Something about the sound made me feel uneasy and my stomach gave an unexpected lurch.

'Are you all right?' Chris asked, concern on his face. 'You've gone white.'

I breathed deeply. 'A really odd feeling just came over me. I'm fine. Maybe we should get that coffee now.'

Chris helped me climb out of the pond and put his arm around my waist as we walked back to the house. He settled me at the kitchen table and bustled about making the drinks, but I noticed him glancing at me surreptitiously every now and then, as though he was expecting me to collapse. Once I was in the house, though, I felt fine. Whatever it was had passed.

That night, I couldn't sleep. The wind howled around the house, rattling the windows and screeching through the trees until, defeated, I swung my legs out of bed, intending to go downstairs and get a drink. As I sat on the side of the bed, I saw a faint glow on the curtains, so I crossed to the window and peered out.

There was a strange, luminous fog hovering over the end of the garden. I squinted, puzzled. It looked like the delicate mist I had seen over lakes and rivers, but there was no water in the pond yet. I dropped the curtain and rubbed my eyes, then looked out again. It was pitch black.

I caught my breath and leaned forwards, trying to work out what was going on. All at once, a face appeared in front of me outside the window. It was so sudden and so horrible that I let out a scream of fright and staggered backwards. I collided with the bed and landed half on top of Chris. He woke with a yell and fumbled for the light switch. The room was bathed in a soft glow as he caught hold of me and turned me to face him.

'What? What is it? Are you OK?' he demanded, reaching up to brush my hair out of my eyes. I stared at him, my mouth opening and closing, but the words wouldn't come. Chris looked across at the curtains, so innocuous. 'Was there someone in the garden?'

I nodded, then shook my head, still trying to form words. Chris's eyes flitted from me to the curtains and I could tell he was on high alert.

'Look at me, Sophie,' he said, his voice firm but gentle. 'It's OK. What did you see?'

The words broke free at last. 'A face,' I gasped. My hands were shaking uncontrollably. 'Right outside the window.'

'A face?' he repeated, folding me into an embrace. 'Sweetheart, I think you've had a nightmare. It would have been your reflection.'

I pushed him away, frustrated. 'Don't patronise me, Chris. It was not my reflection!' I exclaimed.

'It must have been.'

'He had a beard, Chris!' His eyes widened at that. He leapt out of bed, ran to the window and flung the curtains back, but there was no sign of the face.

'Stay here,' he said, heading for the door. I leaped up and grabbed him.

'Where are you going?' I quavered.

'I'm just going to have a quick check downstairs,' he said, trying to prise his arm from my grasp.

'No, Chris, please stay here,' I begged. 'My phone is in my bag. We can call the police.'

He regarded me for a moment. 'I'm just going to check the doors,' he said, his voice reassuring and calm. 'We need to be sure someone is out there before we bother the police.'

'I'm not lying!' I insisted, tears threatening.

'I didn't say you were, sweetheart,' he said, pulling me to him and kissing my forehead. 'Let me look around and then we can decide what to do. You stay in here. OK?'

Without waiting for an answer, he gently loosened my grip on his arm and left the room. He ran downstairs while I huddled in the bed, eyes fixed on the window and the duvet pulled up to my chin. All at once, the house was silent, oppressive. Why couldn't I hear Chris? Had something happened to him? My heart slammed against my ribs as I sat there in an agony of fear. Chris had not closed the curtains and I was terrified that the face would appear again, rising from below the window frame to fix me with its malevolent eyes.

I felt horribly exposed in the glow from the bedside lamp. Panic rose in my throat as I realised that whoever was out there might be able to see me, but I was too scared to get up and close the curtains. All at once, I heard Chris clattering about downstairs and my heart pounded even faster. There was the sound of lights switching on, of doors opening and closing, of his footsteps as he went from room to room. When he came back into the bedroom, I released a breath I was not aware I'd been holding.

He went to the window again and peered out, his nose almost touching the glass.

'Everything's fine downstairs. Turn the light off for a moment, sweetheart,' he said. I reached across with a shaking hand and flipped the switch, plunging us both into darkness.

Nothing happened.

Chris stayed at the window for several minutes. He opened it and we both listened intently, but all we could hear was the soft, velvet rustling of the trees at the end of the garden as a gentle breeze swirled through the leaves.

I was about to tell Chris to come back to bed when a loud, shrill bark rent the air. We both started violently and I let out a whimper of fright. Chris was beside me in an instant, his arms wrapped tightly around me. 'It's OK,' he soothed. 'It's just a fox barking.'

I managed a smile of relief as he switched the light back on and went to draw the curtains. There was nothing outside but our beautiful garden and, beyond, the silhouette of the glorious Devon landscape, inky black against the bruise-coloured sky.

The following morning, we both went around the garden to see if there was anything amiss. Over breakfast, I had told Chris exactly what I'd seen – the mist as well as the man's face. Although I could tell he was deeply sceptical and thought I had been caught up in an incredibly realistic nightmare, he took my hand and led me down to the pond.

It was fine. The garden was unchanged and as welcoming as usual. The outside of the house was secure, the garage untouched. Whatever I had seen, it had done us no harm. And, as Chris pointed out, there was no way that someone could have been directly outside our window without a ladder.

'We'd have heard them setting it up, or heard them climbing,' he said. 'And I'd have definitely either heard or seen something when I was downstairs if there had been someone in the garden collapsing a ladder and running off with it.'

I managed a small smile. My logical mind told me he was right. 'It seemed so real,' I said. 'I'm sorry I ruined your night.'

He hugged me and tilted my chin up so he could kiss me. 'As long as you're OK,' he said. 'That's the main thing.'

He went off to work and I settled down in my study to edit the chapter I'd written a couple of days earlier. After about an hour, I pushed my chair back and stared at the pages, unable to concentrate. Coffee was needed after my disturbed night, I decided. I went down to the kitchen and switched the kettle on. As it started to heat up, I went to the back door and looked out over the garden. Everything was as serene and beautiful as ever. I smiled and took a deep, satisfied breath, already feeling better. There was an odd tang in the air – earthy, unpleasant. I wondered why I hadn't noticed it before.

I turned away from the door and there was a man in the kitchen.

He was huge. Tall, filthy, wearing a long, rough coat. He stank of decay. His face was contorted into a snarl and his hands were reaching for my throat. As I screamed, he vanished.

I fell back against the door, feeling terror beyond anything I had ever known. My knees gave way and I sank to the floor, shaking. What was going on?

One thing I knew for certain, though. The twisted, grimacing face was the same one I had seen at the window last night.

~ ~ ~ ~

I don't know how long I sat on the floor. It could have been minutes. It could have been an hour. My heart thumped so hard I thought it was going to burst out of my chest. I couldn't think straight and my breathing came in short, panicked gasps that made me dizzy. When the doorbell rang, I screamed again. Whoever was outside started hammering on the front door and I froze. Should I open the door? Was I in danger? Maybe it was the postman. I would be safe with him. I hauled myself to my feet and half-staggered, half-crawled along the hall to the door.

It was Trevor Smith. He eyed me curiously as I clung to the door, staring at him. I realised my face was a mess of tears. I wiped it with the back of my hand, but he stopped me and, without a word, he reached into his pocket and held out a handkerchief. I took it gratefully and mopped at my face.

'Things've been 'appening, haven't they?' Trevor asked matter-of-factly. When I stared at him in shock, he nodded. 'Thought so. Can I come in?'

145

'Wait,' I began, but he gently manoeuvred me out of the way and strode into the hall, looking around him. When he reached the kitchen doorway, he stopped and gave a couple of sharp sniffs. I didn't know what was the most frightening - the thing I had seen in the kitchen, the village drunk barging his way into my home, or the fact that he seemed to know something about what was going on. After a moment, in which my confused thoughts swirled around in my head like moths in headlights, I closed the front door and trailed after Trevor. He was in the kitchen by then, still sniffing the air.

'I told 'ee,' he said when I joined him. He didn't reek of alcohol for once, which was a relief.

'Trevor, you can't just push your way in here,' I tried, my voice weak. He narrowed his eyes as he looked at me.

'What did you see?' he asked.

'I don't ...'

'Look, I know you've see'd something, young lady. What was it?'

What little strength I had ebbed away and I sank into a chair, leaning my elbows on the table and cradling my head in my hands. 'I don't know what's happening, Trevor.'

He pulled out a chair and sat opposite me. 'Just tell me straight,' he said. I looked at him. I had only ever spoken to him that one time, yet here he was, in my kitchen, just when I needed someone. After a moment's hesitation, I told him.

When I got to the part about the face at the window, he blanched, but said nothing. When I described the man I had just seen in the kitchen, he got up and started pacing.

'You've let 'im out,' he said. 'You've gone and let 'im out.'

'Let who out? And out of where?'

Trevor wheeled round, making me cringe back in my chair. 'I told 'ee!' he exclaimed. 'I told 'ee that night in the pub. Didn't listen, did 'ee?'

'I'm sorry,' I stammered. 'What you were saying didn't make sense ...'

'Bloody incomers,' he muttered, turning his gaze onto the garden. All at once, he stiffened. 'What's that over there?' he demanded, jerking a thumb towards where Chris had been digging.

'We're putting a pond in,' I said.

Trevor immediately tried to open the back door, but it was locked. He hovered impatiently while I fumbled with the keys. As soon as the door was open, he was off, running down the length of the garden and skidding to a stop at the edge of the pond. I hurried after him, bewildered. What on earth was he doing? I wondered if I ought to call Chris and get him to come home. I wasn't sure I could handle Trevor on my own.

Trevor was looking all around the garden now, his eyes narrowed, and it seemed like he was counting under his breath as his eyes moved from tree to tree. He started making gestures with his hands as though he was doing calculations in his head. All at once, he let his hands drop and turned to face me.

'What did 'ee find in the ground?' he asked.

'Find?' I repeated. 'Nothing. We just dug the hole for the pond. We didn't find anything.'

'Yes, you did,' he insisted.

I was about to protest when I recalled the strange metal object, so I told him about it. Before I'd finished, he interrupted me.

'Where is it?' he asked. 'What've 'ee done with it?'

'Chris threw it over there,' I said, pointing. 'We were going to take it to the tip.'

Trevor hurried over and started scouring the area, finally giving a low cry of satisfaction. He reached down, then hesitated, his fingers twitching just above the object. He straightened up and stared at it for a long moment, rubbing his chin. 'Think I'd better get vicar.'

'The vicar?' I gasped, wondering if I'd heard him right. 'Whatever for?'

But he was already fishing in a pocket for his phone, muttering something unintelligible when he realised there was no service. 'I needs to use your phone,' he stated. 'Urgent, like.'

Wordlessly I led him back inside and sat in the kitchen while he rang the vicar from the house phone. Fifteen minutes later, the doorbell rang and I opened the door to find the vicar, out of breath, on my welcome mat.

I am not particularly religious and had never met the vicar before. The Reverend Peter Andrews was a tall, austere man in his late fifties and he looked worried. After a brief introduction and even briefer handshake, I showed him into the garden, where Trevor was standing as though on guard.

'Trevor,' the vicar said by way of greeting.

'Thanks for coming, Peter. They've only gone and let 'im out,' said Trevor, with an accusing glance at me. I felt heat flare in my cheeks as the vicar cast a baleful look at me. He turned back to Trevor.

'Didn't you warn them?' he asked.

'Excuse me, gentlemen, but I'm standing right here in *my* garden,' I reminded them. 'What are you talking about?'

'A long time ago,' the vicar began, 'there used to be a mansion on the hill over there, about two miles away.' He gestured. 'All of this area was just beyond the estate walls. The family was called Langley. In the 1500s, the lord of the manor, Charles Langley, had been visiting friends on the North Devon coast. He

148

rode home across Exmoor. Something happened on that journey. Almost overnight, his temperament changed and he became volatile and prone to violent outbursts. The coachman who had driven him left his post the next day and moved to another parish.'

I was growing impatient. What on earth did this have to do with the terrible experiences I had had? I opened my mouth but the vicar held up his hand and I subsided.

'One night, the household was awakened by screaming. Langley had cornered one of the housemaids in the drawing room and had bitten her on the neck. When the family found them, Langley appeared to be drinking the girl's blood.'

The hairs stood up on the back of my neck and I gasped as a shudder raced down my spine.

'The local magistrate was sent for, along with a couple of constables, but by the time they reached Langley Hall, Charles had disappeared. The family had secured him in his room, or so they thought, but he had somehow managed to escape through the window. No one knows how, for his room was on the second floor and there was no tree nearby, or anything that he could have used to climb down. That was how the rumours began.'

'Rumours?' I asked, my curiosity overtaking my impatience.

'Over the next few nights, Langley was seen in the village,' the vicar continued, glancing about him uncomfortably. 'There were twenty-seven incidents during that time. People were attacked, bitten, their blood drunk. Everyone believed Langley to be a vampire. So they all got together, cornered him and killed him. Then they sent for every priest in the adjoining parishes to come and deal with the body. Charles Langley was buried at a crossroads just beyond the edge of the village, with all the priests in attendance, to ensure that he never rose from his grave. Lady Langley, when she had recovered from her shock, went one step further. To keep people safe, she had a new road built which by-passed the crossroads, then planted the entire area with trees and absorbed it into the family's estate. After that, it went quiet and Langley has been safely in the ground ever since. Until now.'

'What?' I blurted out.

'After Charles's death, the Langleys' reputation suffered. When Geoffrey, the heir, came of age and inherited his title, he was already a heavy drinker. He got a taste for gambling and lost everything. The land was sold off piece by piece, the Hall burned down and eventually, there was nothing left. The Langleys ended their days in poverty. It was a tragic story.'

He lapsed into silence. I couldn't think of anything to say, so I just waited, my mind racing and a horrible dread slowly inching its way over me.

'Over time, the Langley woodlands were cut down acre by acre, especially during times of war when wood was needed for ship building, as it was mostly oak and elm. This garden was once at the very edge of the Langley estate.'

'Oh no,' I said, feeling numb. I knew where this was leading. 'He's here, isn't he? I have a body buried in my garden!'

My knees gave way and I sank to the ground again. The vicar hurried over to help me, but I was already kneeling in the grass, trying not to retch, by the time he reached me. I turned panicked eyes to him. 'What do we do?' I asked. 'Do we call the police?'

'No!'

I started violently at Trevor's vehement exclamation.

'All right, Trevor, calm down,' said the vicar. He turned back to me. 'Sophie ... did you disturb any bones when you dug your pond?'

'Bones? No, no ... if we had, we'd have called the police already,' I said, my voice sounding oddly distant and echoey. 'The only strange thing we found was that metal rod.'

'Over 'ere, Peter,' said Trevor, indicating with a nod of his head. The vicar went over and examined it, his face tense.

'Can you show me where this came from?' he asked. 'It needs to be the exact spot.'

We tugged the pond lining aside and I showed him.

'Right, this is what we need to do,' the vicar said in a business-like tone. 'When Langley was buried, the priests staked him in his grave so he couldn't come back. It looks like you found the stake and released him. We need to replace it.'

I stared at him. This was beyond my comprehension. Vampires? Stakes? I had never heard of Devon having any vampire legends before. Was this really happening?

The vicar reached into his pocket and brought out a Bible and a small bottle of clear liquid, which I took to be holy water. 'Now, Sophie, do you have a hammer or a mallet?'

'I ... er, yes, in the garage,' I said. 'I'll get it.'

'Thank you,' the vicar said. 'We need to bless this metal stake and hammer it back into the spot you dug it from.'

I nodded, not really understanding much of what was happening. Like a sleep-walker, I unlocked the garage, found the mallet and went back to the two men. The vicar was sprinkling the stake with the holy water and reciting something in Latin. Then he turned and did the same to the exposed earth at the bottom of the pond. He picked up the stake, took the mallet from me and jumped down into the pond, still reciting the Latin. Digging some of the earth out, he pushed the stake in, glancing up at me as he recited, looking for confirmation. I nodded.

He hit the stake with the mallet.

A sudden gust of wind blew up around us and I couldn't help but cry out in fright, for I could see that nothing else in the garden was moving. How could that be?

The vicar hit the stake again and there arose a volley of whispers. 'You cannot hold me! I see you! I see everything!' They grew ever louder until both Trevor and I had to cover our ears. Trevor's eyes were wide with fear and all I could do was cower on the ground, trying to make myself as small as possible. 'It isn't working,' I thought in a panic.

The wind increased, swirling round us like a straitjacket. The trees swayed and dipped violently and I was terrified that one of them would come crashing down on us. Trevor was knocked off his feet and even the vicar, kneeling at the bottom of the pond, was struggling to keep his balance. I could see the grim determination on his face as he gave the mallet four more blows, five, six ... how many was it going to take? He kept going as the whispers became screams and the screams became howls. Nine. Ten. Then silence.

The wind vanished as suddenly as it had appeared and the silence was heavy, thick and cloying, uncomfortable in its perfection. There was no birdsong, no traffic noise, nothing.

There was a strange, almost physical *whooshing* sound and the atmosphere transformed. Immediately, the air became light and fresh, a blackbird trilled its song from one of the trees and a motorbike growled past, its deep throaty roar filling the air before gradually fading away.

Trevor picked himself up and nodded at the vicar. 'Nicely done,' he panted.

The vicar got up slowly and stared down at the top of the stake. 'I suggest we put an extra layer of earth over it, then perhaps some more of the lining,' he said, a slight tremor in his voice. 'Do you have any more?'

I actually smiled.

~ ~ ~ ~

Once that was done and the two of them had helped me restore the pond to its former appearance, they sat in the kitchen while I made coffee.

'You'm one of us now,' Trevor said suddenly, looking at me over the top of his mug.

'I'm what?' I asked.

'You'm one of us,' he repeated. 'Now you knows. So you share the responsibility with the rest of us who knows.'

'Responsibility?' I had no idea what he was talking about.

'There are a few of us in the village who are aware of the story,' the vicar said, spooning sugar into his coffee. 'We act as guardians, I suppose. Both of the village itself and of...' He tailed off, his gaze turning towards the garden. 'Of that. Of Langley. It's up to us to ensure that he never gets out again. You're part of that now. Can we rely on you?'

I thought of the horror I had been through. Something unspeakable was buried at the bottom of my garden and I had seen it face to face. I agreed that it needed to be contained, whatever it was, but my first instinct was to run away from my dream home and never come back. I was also worried that there might be unpleasant repercussions if it was discovered that there was a body buried in my garden, but who was I going to tell? Should I tell Chris? I trusted him completely and knew that he would keep the secret, but his experience was different to mine. He hadn't seen what I'd seen. Would it be better to keep it to myself? I looked at Trevor and the vicar. They were both watching me, their faces serious and intense.

'Yes,' I said, my voice firm. 'Yes, you can rely on me.'

We finished our drinks in silence, then Trevor and the vicar rose to leave. I went with them as far as the front gate. The vicar gave me his card as he left and I caught his arm, surprising myself.

'How do you know all this?' I asked in a low voice. 'I've never heard of a vampire in Devon before. Is it in a book?'

The vicar's lips thinned a little and it was Trevor who answered.

'Ain't in no book,' he said. 'Peter's mother and my father were descended from the Langleys' young daughter. Charles Langley was our ancestor.'

Stunned, I watched them go, one tall and upright, the other shambling. I went back into the house and closed the door, leaning against it as I sampled the atmosphere. Had the house changed? Was there any lingering trace of that awful figure?

No. It was as warm and comforting and peaceful as it had always been. All I could smell was coffee and a slight touch of furniture polish.

I let out a huge sigh of relief and went back to the kitchen table to wait for Chris to come home.

Winter Snow
By Chip Tolson

Amelia woke with a jolt. Zoe, her daughter, already dressed and excited, had run into her room jumping onto the bed.

'Here comes your breakfast.'

'It's only a mug of tea, Zoe and don't jump on the bed; Aunt Amelia might bounce out.' Kate, the oldest of Amelia's nieces and nephews looked after Zoe when they came to Devon to stay at Stonebarrow Farm. Kate's two younger brothers, the twins, lingered in the corridor looking round the bedroom door uncertain whether it was right to barge into their aunt's bedroom.

'Please don't call me 'Aunt'. It makes me feel old. Is that bacon I smell cooking?'

'Yes, you can come down in your dressing gown and have a bath afterwards.'

'I'll get dressed. Let me have my tea and then I'll race you all downstairs.'

Sarah heard the thunder of feet moments before the kitchen door burst open.

'Whatever are you all doing?'

'Sorry, it's my fault,' Amelia laughed.

'You're all as bad as each other. Have you recovered from your drive, Amelia?'

'I feel great. Is there coffee?'

'In the pot on the stove.'

'We're all going swimming later; can you swim, Amelia?' Kate asked.

'Like a fish, but I'm going for a long walk this morning to clear away my urban cobwebs.'

Sarah and the children set off for the swimming pool in the battered Land Rover after breakfast, Zoe, the baby of the pack, happy in the care of her cousin Kate.

Amelia strode off with Echo, the farm dog, bounding ahead into the fields heading toward woodlands bordering a stream. Wearing a heavy coat over a thick sweater against the morning frost, she rejoiced in the sunshine, taking in the view over Devon's folding winter hills, ribbed with a lattice of hedgerows linking scattered farms nested in their hillside footprints. London, its commuting and her hectic City desk, seemed an age away.

'Thank God for Stonebarrow Farm,' Amelia shouted startling a pair of pigeons erupting from the kale with a clatter of wings. Overhead a buzzard banked on invisible currents mewing as it quartered the valley. With cacophonous calls and throbbing flight, pheasants burst out of the hillside gorse half a field away as the dog worked the cover.

In their airy farm shed, cattle munched chopped silage. Andrew relished the eagerness of his cows pushing against the barrier as fresh rations were tipped from the feeding trailer. He had a name for every beast, all bred on the farm, each one a step toward their planned Stonebarrow organic beef herd. He needed to stay close to the sheds today, another calf was due.

Andrew walked across the yard seeing Echo in the distance racing in circles round his kid sister. He smiled before making for the kitchen to kick off his boots in the scullery, amused at the mix of depth and childish fun in his younger sibling.

Her work in the deeper recesses of a merchant bank was demanding, but it paid an extraordinary salary; more in a year than he could make in a decade from the three hundred acres of the family hill farm. Yet there she was running across the fields as if just off the school bus forgetting about her homework.

A cat in the chair by the stove yawned, stretched its forelegs out and went back to sleep.

~ ~ ~ ~

Exhausted by running, Amelia looked back toward the farm. Dark lowering clouds were piling high blowing in from the north. She turned to search along an old hedgerow bank bordering the woodland, keen to find the first signs of spring amongst the winter-bleached vegetation.

Snow came, first only a few flakes, later billowing in the wind until the field was whiting over, driving her to shelter. Amelia called Echo, they squelched in slushy mud through a gateway to find shelter in the woodland. For a while she sat leaning against the trunk of an old oak, huddling close with the dog, wet and muddy from the fields. Windblown snow seeped in amongst the trees, dampening her hair, settling on her coat.

After a while she couldn't see the field. The dog shivered and started to whimper.

'Come on, Echo, before we're covered. Let's go home.'

Snow swirled round, confusing their path. Amelia walked for a while but didn't find the hedge bank, or the gate. The dog, its head down, trailed behind, then spooked as Amelia lost her footing to tumble down a snow hidden rocky slope.

Amelia lay unmoving, a whirling sensation befuddling her mind, a ribbon of blood running down her cheek; utter stillness pervading the woodland.

A face peered down at her from far away. As she focused it came closer, then there were two, dark-eyed swarthy faces, staring into her soul. She stirred, they backed away, unblinking, puzzled, looking deep into her blue eyes. She wanted to get up, but as she tried to rise a pain shot from her ankle to her back and she fell.

She didn't hit the ground, grasped in an embrace of coarse clothed arms.

~ ~ ~ ~

The swimmers ate fish and chips from a café on the seafront then played running games on the beach until it was time to go home. The aged Land Rover climbed into the hills running into snow, the children's excitement steaming the windows, Sarah bent forward to wipe the windscreen with her glove. The blower was broken.

In the kitchen, Sarah slid the kettle across the stove onto the hot plate. 'Get a cake and biscuits from the larder, Kate,' she told her daughter as she went out to the sheds to find her husband.

'Has the calf come?'

'Not yet, it won't be long now. Were you OK in the snow?'

'The weather was fine down at the beach. We ran into it half way back, it's slippery on the top road. Has Amelia been with you?'

'I haven't seen her since she went out with Echo this morning.'

'I didn't see her indoors. She must be upstairs catching up with sleep.' Sarah turned back to the house. 'There's tea and cake on the table when you have a moment.'

She made the tea, settling the children round the table before pouring a mug to take up to Amelia.

~ ~ ~ ~

'Andrew, I've looked everywhere. There's no sign of Amelia.'

'She must be here somewhere.'

'The wellies she borrowed are not by the back door. I've searched upstairs. She isn't here.'

'Where's the dog?'

'Echo isn't here either.'

'I saw her in the yard earlier, looking cowed with her tail between her legs.' Andrew went to look for the dog. He found her in the outside kennel, lurking at the back, silent and shivering. He called her out, she wouldn't move.

'Where's Mummy?' Zoe was clutching a half-eaten slice of cake and holding two seagull feathers from the beach.

'She must have gone for another walk, Zoe.'

'I think she'll be back soon,' said Zoe taking another bite from her cake.

Sarah beckoned Kate out of the room. 'Look after Zoe and the boys. Amelia should have been back ages ago. Daddy and I will go out to look for her.' Sarah smiled at her daughter.

'Don't worry. I'll look after the children.'

Sarah gave her a hug. Her daughter was growing up too fast.

~ ~ ~ ~

Andrew's lamp was useless reflecting off the blizzard. For a while he heard Sarah calling round the buildings but making his way further from the farm her voice was soaked up in the blanket of snow. What could have scared the dog to flee back home leaving Amelia? He looked at his watch, he'd looked at it several times in the last hour. It took him twenty more minutes to get back to the loom of the yard lights.

'Any joy?'

'Nothing, I got down to the stream and then back along the woodland, it's a whiteout.'

'She isn't anywhere round here. But you've got a fine bull calf.'

'Did the cow need help?'

'No. I didn't see it at first in the straw. I'm sure he wasn't there when I first looked.'

'We need to get a search party organized.'

~ ~ ~ ~

Wood smoke curled through roof timbers seeping out through a gap in the thatch, flames sparked as logs were thrown on the fire, a sea of faces came close reaching rough hands to her face, touching her fair hair in disbelief. There was a smell of woodsmoke and bodies, hard worked bodies mixed with the scent of herbs.

An old woman, her skin gaunt and wrinkled round deep-set eyes, stared into her face. The woman chewed, took plant stems from her toothless gums to lay a masticated poultice onto Amelia's wound, easing her throbbing head. Coarse cloth rubbed against her shivering skin helpless to move.

The young men laid her down near a bearded figure staring with golden eyes, the young men were pushed away; women gathered round.

The bearded figure watched in silence. The women moved back. The figure nodded, reached forward to place soft hands on her face. Furs were laid over her and her shivering stopped. The bearded figure passed something to the old woman; she knelt and fastened the object around Amelia's neck. A bunch of herbs was held to her face, rubbed by unseen fingers releasing their heady fragrance.

~ ~ ~ ~

Snow carpeted the fields as daylight crept over the landscape; Amelia forced herself to run, only stopping as she reached the edge of the woodland, pain surging through her leg. She leant against a beech tree's smooth bark regaining her breath and only then did she look back. She was alone. Seeing where she was, she limped from the woodland, her borrowed wellies squelching through the slush.

She started back toward the farm stumbling through the drifted snow; the adrenaline from her flight spent.

Andrew raced his tractor over the field.

'Thank God, whatever happened to you?' Andrew jumped down seeing the wound on her forehead and hugged her. 'Come on we must get you home.'

'I'm sorry, Andrew. Is Zoe all right?'

'She's fine.'

~ ~ ~ ~

There was commotion back at the farmhouse. Amelia sat in the kitchen by the stove, absorbing warmth, smelling coffee and toast, bacon and eggs sizzled in the frying pan. A policeman and the overnight search team waited to tuck into breakfast. Echo was happy to be in the midst of the throng of people, sitting by Amelia licking her hand.

She wanted to tell them what had happened even if she couldn't make any sense of the delirious saga of her night; there were no words to describe it, other than she fell and lost consciousness in the snowstorm.

Doctor Gregg arrived to check the patient. 'Sarah, get Amelia bathed and into bed. If her headache persists then I'll want to see her again.'

The wound on the patient's forehead puzzled him, broken skin, purple bruising, it was nasty but it had been dressed in some way with what he took to be herbs. It smelt sweet, but there'd be no herbs to pick in the wood at this time of year and she didn't look as if she had been out all night.

Amelia lay deep in bubbles in the huge farmhouse bathroom, fiddling with a piece of carved antler as she soaked in the hot water. Sarah sat in an armchair by the bathroom window, while Kate gently brushed Amelia's long blonde hair over the back of the bath, taking care not to aggravate the wound on her aunt's forehead. Zoe's seagull feathers were stuck into a piece of soap on the shelf by the bath; the child tried to wrap a hanky as a bandage round her doll's head, then asked to see the newborn calf in the sheds.

'Don't let Zoe and the twins get cold, Kate. Wrap up well.'

'We will.' Kate called back from the landing.

The two women looked at each other.

'You're not going to believe me.'

'Try me.'

~ ~ ~ ~

Days later, with Amelia back in the cut and thrust of corporate City life, Andrew and Sarah sat round the kitchen table with Dr Sandy Gregg and Lizzy, his wife.

Sarah had been reluctant to tell them Amelia's story. The doctor, puzzled by Amelia's condition after her night in the blizzard, persuaded her.

'The wound on her forehead had been dressed with an herbal treatment, I don't know what, but it was beneficial.' The doctor fiddled with the stem of his wine glass as he spoke. 'I don't think she'd put ointment on herself.'

Sarah told them Amelia's story, about the two dark eyed men dressed in coarse woven garments who'd carried her into shelter, of the women who'd cared for her by a fire wrapping her in furs and the old woman who had chewed leaves and dressed her wound.

She told them just as Amelia had told it, about the bearded man dressed in finery, how he'd touched her cheek, how he'd given the piece of carved antler to the old woman to tie round her neck; how as it got light she had run till her lungs were bursting.

'Her clothes were dry.' Dr Sandy was frowning. 'She was out all the night in the blizzard and her clothes were dry and smelt of woodsmoke.'

'It sounds like one of her yarns to me. Amelia always made up stories as a child,' Andrew gave a chuckle. 'She would come back from one of her rambles swearing she'd been talking with fairies. I don't know about not looking like she had been out all night, but she did the Duke of Edinburgh's Gold badge, she knows a thing or two about staying out in all weathers. I only got the Bronze.'

'Did you say she still had a piece of antler with her when she got back?' Lizzy asked.

'Yes, she gave it to Kate.'

'I'd like to see it.

'I'll get it; more coffee, anyone?'

~ ~ ~ ~

Kate was asleep; Sarah found the piece of antler, suspended on a cord her daughter had laced through a carved hole, hanging from the mirror on her chest of drawers.

For a while Lizzy looked at the piece, feeling the marks carved into it with her fingers, before passing it to her husband. He held it letting it dangle in his grasp before passing it back.

'Well?' Sarah looked across at her guests. 'What is it?'

Lizzy turned it over looking at its detail with an eye glass taken from her bag, inspecting the carvings. 'I don't know, but... it's certainly old, very old,' she paused. 'I went on a lot of digs when I was a student. I've seen something like this before. The pattern of the carving is believed to hold meaning. Do you remember, Sandy? On that dig I took you to at Duizenheim in Westphalia, when we were students?'

'And it rained all the time, it does look the same.'

'What do you think it is?' asked Sarah.

'Remnants of others like it have been found in barrows, with burials from the Bronze Age. I don't know about here in Devon, nor how Amelia could have found it; I suppose some animal might have dug it out of the ground and she picked it up.'

'Was it a mark of rank or something?'

'No one is certain; there is a theory pieces like this were worn by chosen ones when these tribes made sacrifices to their Gods.'

'You mean human sacrifices?'

Lizzie shrugged her shoulders. 'When the summer comes, it would be an idea to get into your woodland to do a bit of a search. There may be something interesting in there, signs of a Bronze Age settlement.'

The Padding Horror
By Mark Norman

There were only four people in my life of any importance to me. Just four. Three of them are now gone, plucked from my life and from existence itself by that infernal animal. Only Cassandra is left. And so, I must do this to save her the same fate. The universe must take me, so that the creature cannot take her. Only I, alone, can stop them. For I have found their portal. That liminal boundary, the gateway between this universe and theirs, is here in the bowels of this unassuming cottage hospital. And I believe I can close the gap.

What will happen to me, I cannot tell. Truth to tell, it matters not. If it wipes me from existence in this realm, then so be it. It is a small price to pay. If they take me, then she may remain. That is all that matters. Dear, sweet Cassandra may continue to live her blameless life. And the Dog can go and hunt for souls in some other corner of the sphere: some other plane of existence far from me ... and far from her.

But we must begin at the beginning.

I have lived all my life in a small cottage on the edge of Chagford Common. It is a remote, wild place at times and it takes a hardy soul to exist there on the extremes of Dartmoor. But exist there we do. Or at least, we did. My father was a sheep farmer, keeping stock upon the common. My mother tended the family home and washed and spun fleece to sell in the local market. And my poor sister, Emily, not long out of her schooling, would run errands for us all whilst she learnt the ways of the world from my parents.

My first experience of the Dog was on a wild winter's night some three months ago. The wind had a bitter chill, I recall, and we had retired early, for it was not a night to be out. The rain had battered relentlessly on the window panes of the cottage, but being well used to such weather, I had drifted off easily enough into a dreamless sleep.

It was just before two in the morning when I was awoken by the strangest, most unearthly sounds from the common in the distance. This I know, for the old grandfather clock in the hall broke off briefly from its relentless tick...tick...tick to chime the two knolls of the hour.

As the sound of the bell reverberated away to nothing and the pendulum once again continued counting time ever onwards, the sound from outside came again. It was carried on the strong wind of the storm, but it was a howling not like any that the wind around the chimney cowls and eaves created, for I had heard those oft enough through many winters as the moor threw all of its might at the house for nights on end.

This howling was not natural. It was animalistic and yet, somehow, unlike any animal that I had heard before. Surrounded as we are by sheep, cattle and the hardy Dartmoor ponies I was well versed with their sounds, both in pleasure or in pain, and it was none of these. It was canine and yet, somehow, not. It began as the howl of a normal dog, of a large size judging by the tone, but it continued – developed into something more. Something foreboding. Something horrific. Something ... infernal.

I sat up in bed, quite awake now, and listened intently to the noise. It had, I thought, sounded quite distant when it began but as the sound changed, moulding itself from a dog to something indescribable, it got louder. It was as if it was approaching the cottage and yet, nothing else seemed to stir. I could see the flock in the distance, wind-battered and wet, yet grazing as normal. As the volume of the sound increased and it began to appear as if some demon was being sent from another world, the atmosphere itself seemed to change. The air felt thicker somehow, as if it were closing in around me.

I could feel my heart rate rising as the infernal noise from outside, whining, howling, screaming almost, appeared to get nearer and nearer. At last, just as I thought that my ears could stand to hear it no longer, there came an almighty crash against the old glass panes of the bedroom window, as if the creature itself had flung itself at the casement. I threw my hands over my face, instinctively shielding myself from the force of the glass that was inevitably going to be flung into the room.

And then nothing. Silence, save the still blowing wind and the tick ... tick ... tick of the old clock, steadily counting the seconds away. I dropped my hands to my sides and looked up. The window remained shut fast, unbroken and firm. No glass. No damage. No creature.

I sat in bed for some minutes, contemplating what had just occurred, before I rose and crossed to the window. Looking out of the casement into the darkness, I listened to the wind as it continued to whip around the outside of the cottage, battering the glass with detritus whipped up from the ground.

I returned to my mattress and sank back, pulling the thin covers over me. What had I just experienced? It could surely not have been just the storm, just a trick of the mind and of the ear. I closed my eyes and thought on the event before finally drifting off into a dreamless repose.

As I sat at breakfast with my family the following morning, I chose to mention nothing of the previous night.

My parents, my father particularly, were simple folk but did not hold with the traditions or lore of the area like so many others. They lived, they worked. Nothing more, nothing less. So instead I sat, shared in the simple repast of the morning and then set out on the day's errands. Being a market day, I had need to take the horse and cart across the moor to Tavistock. It was a journey I made every week, shared with my good friend Stevenson, who also bought and sold wares in the town. He was less closed of mind than my family and I resolved to question him on the subject as we made the drive.

'Fascinating,' Stevenson expounded some two hours later as we sat atop the cart, the old horse clopping its way steadily over the well worn track toward Tavistock. 'You know, of course, of the Yeth Hounds?'

I assured him that I did not and he proceeded to tell me of the legend of great black hounds, said to accompany a phantasmal hunting party on wild nights such as we had just experienced. They say, according to Stevenson, that a Devil leads the hunt and that a party of other creatures ride alongside. Stevenson referred to them as 'lesser demons', though the term seemed strange to me and I did not remember any such thing from the scant bible classes which I had been forced to attend in my younger days.

Stevenson scoffed at the idea. 'The bible does not account for all in this world, my friend,' he said. 'There are creatures, places, far beyond any that may be found in those pages. The Book of Revelation is probably all that comes close. John - being the author of those words - evidently knew more than most.'

His words seemed odd to me, and I was about to question him further on them, when he continued.

'I think there is something in town that might interest you,' he said. 'We will go there after the market. No more until then.'

And indeed he spoke no more on the subject. We crossed the moor on an uneventful drive, visited the market and, having undertaken all those jobs which we had set out to do, found ourselves with a spare couple of hours before we needed to head back.

Stevenson took me to the Bedford Hotel and told me that the function room was currently in use for the display of a travelling exhibition of antiquities and oddities that had been collected from around the country. I wondered what the relevance of this was, but explaining that I would find out soon enough he led on and I soon found myself in a room full of curios. Ignoring all of these, Stevenson led me to a cabinet at the back of the room which had been turned into a form of makeshift library. It was here that was located the item which he evidently thought important.

'This is what I wanted you to see,' he said, pulling from the cabinet an ancient looking tome which he laid upon the table in front of us. 'This is called the Anglo Saxon Chronicle,' he explained. 'It is a kind of official history of old England. It was written for one of the kings in years past. This is not the original,' he continued, 'but rather one of the copies.'

Stevenson went on to explain that the original document was sent, about a thousand years past, to monasteries around the country where copies were made. These copies were kept in different towns, and the monks continued to update them with such events as they thought important.

'This one comes from a town called Peterborough,' Stevenson told me. I had not heard of it but he said that it was in the North of England somewhere. 'They say,' he continued, 'that the abbot of this particular monastery was very disreputable. Nobody knows for certain what was going on there, but there are some very strange things recorded in this book. Things not of this world, but another. This is the bit that I thought would be important.'

He leafed through the pages, looking for a particular passage to show me. Finally, his hand fell upon the paragraph that he was looking for. I looked, but there were no words upon the page. At least, nothing that I recognised as words in any case.

'It is written in the native tongue,' he said. 'But I can read it to you.'

Now, I freely admit that Stevenson is a more learned man that I, but I wondered how he was able to read these markings that I did not understand. I asked him, but he just quietened me, saying that it was not important. He bade me listen and then read the passage aloud.

'Many men,' he quoted from the page, 'both saw and heard a great number of huntsmen hunting. The huntsmen were black, huge and hideous, and rode on black horses and on black he-goats and their hounds were black and big eyed and loathsome.'

He closed the book and returned it to the cabinet. 'Come on,' he said with no more explanation. 'You have seen what I needed you to see. Let us go back home.'

Despite my questioning him further on the subject, Stevenson was no more forthcoming with information as we crossed back from Tavistock, past Princetown and over Two Bridges before arriving back in Chagford. He just told me that I needed to have seen the passage, that it was important, and that he was sure that it would hold some meaning for me over the event of the previous night. Eventually I gave up and turned to other subjects before we finally dropped down over the hill and into Chagford. It was getting rather late by the time I had delivered Stevenson home, fed and watered the horse and packed away the goods and chattels from the market and the cottage was in darkness. I could do nothing more that night but retire, still thinking upon the book and the curious words that Stevenson had shown me.

My dreams that night were haunted with strange visions that I did not understand, of galloping horses and strange creatures, of hideous demeanour, sat atop black shaggy-haired animals. And running alongside them, black dogs with large red eyes and strange half-canine, half-human features. Is that the right term? Half-*in*human is more accurate.

The night was restless - not outside the house for, unlike the previous one, it was calm and still - but rather inside, as my mind wrestled with these images. I recall that I woke, at what must have been two or three, thinking that I had heard again those strange sounds from out in the fields. The feeling was strong enough that I lit a lantern and, slipping on some boots and a gown, I went outside to look.

Save the bleating of the sheep in the field, all seemed still and quiet. I rounded the corner of the cottage, towards the area over which my first-floor bedroom looked. The edges of the cottage sink into the earth alongside the clitter of Dartmoor granite. I picked my way along by the light of the lantern until, drawing level with the kitchen window, over which my bedroom was located, I noticed something strange about the ground. This was an area I had trodden many times so, to me, it was obvious when something was not as it usually appeared.

I bent down to take a closer look at the ground beneath my window, extending my arm forwards to cast the light of the lantern around me. There, in the ground within the flickering arc of the lantern's light, was a single footprint. Deep. Clear. Canine.

Long claw marks were clearly visible protruding from the impression of large pads sunken into the mud. Large, in the way that a Shire horse is large when placed next to a Dartmoor pony. I looked around but there were no others leading up to or away from the cottage. Just this single impression in the ground. It made no sense. The ground was wet from the previous night's storm so the other prints should have been clearly visible. I stared at the ground, unable to fully comprehend what I was seeing.

The sudden, loud bleat of a sheep caused me to start and brought me back to reality. I pulled my gown around me, suddenly cold despite the relative mild air of the night and returned to the cottage, not understanding what was happening.

At breakfast the following morning, I sat in silence, pondering, thinking on the events of the last twenty-four hours.

'Wha's up wi' thee?' demanded my father, demolishing what looked like a side of bacon jammed between two doorstop wedges of bread. Reticent about telling him what had happened, knowing what his response was likely to be, I shrugged the question off.

'Don' be daft,' he pressed further, 'thou's 'ad a gert frown on thee since tha got back vrom Tavvy. What's tha bloody miserable 'bout?'

I sighed and relayed the events to him. Emily, sat opposite me at the table, listened intently and when I got to the footprint from just a few hours past, I thought her jaw was going to actually hit the flagstones of the floor. Father grunted and was about to speak when Emily rushed to the window and looked out.

'Where?' she asked. 'Where is it? I don't see nuthin'.'

'Emily. Go an' 'elp ma wi' the pots,' Father scolded. She protested, of course, but was dispatched to the sink. I crossed to the window and looked out, but indeed she was right. The earth outside, though still wet, was flat. There was no footprint. I could not have imagined it, nor dreamed it. I went outside, after all, and I knew this to be true as I could clearly see my own boot prints leading up to the window. I stammered my lack of understanding out loud, to nobody in particular, but my father jumped upon it.

'Enough,' he chastised. 'We don' want to hear no more on't. An' we certainly don' want to hear no more 'bout old books an' the like. You'm daft to think on't. Them things is cursed, most like. An' keep away from Stevenson. He's odd that'n. There's some odd rumours about'n round Chagford.'

I tried to question him on what he meant; what rumours and what about Stevenson? But he would speak no more and I trudged out into the field to tend to the sheep.

That afternoon, I accompanied Emily into town, for she had been sent to order some provisions from the butcher. I wanted to visit dear Cassandra, but knew that I must needs walk Emily back to the cottage after her errand and so would not have the chance. But fate, it seemed, had another deck to deal that afternoon.

We were just leaving the butcher's shop when we bumped into Stevenson in the street.

'Mr Stevenson,' cried Emily, 'my brother, 'ee told me 'bout the noises an' then last night, 'ee went out 'an there were a giant footprint in the earth and now 'tis gone.' She paused for breath at this point, allowing Stevenson to interject with a laugh.

'Slow down, Miss Emily,' he laughed. 'You'll do yourself an injury. Now what's this all about?'

She was about to speak again but I scolded her, telling her that, though not believing such, I had obviously been mistaken and that I must have imagined it. Whatever was happening to me, there was no need to involve Emily, young as she was, in such things.

'Stuff and nonsense,' Stevenson argued. 'There is more to this. You just do not have the knowledge. Come to my house and we will talk further. Bring Emily with you. She will understand.'

I protested, arguing that Emily was young, and impressionable, and trying to make excuses for the things that I had said in front of her. But Stevenson would have none of it. And it was at that point that I realised, for all our years of companionship, that I had never once been to Stevenson's house. We had met frequently, but always on the way to market, or at the inn. But never in his home. I must confess that this fact, and his eagerness, left me more than a little intrigued and so I relented and we walked down the road to his cottage – one of a terrace of small miners' cottages.

As we walked, I explained to Stevenson about the events of the previous night, of the dream and of the footprint. Stevenson remained quiet and attentive until we reached the front door of his house, its paintwork blue and faded from many years of neglect. He turned the old, round wooden handle and with a glance over his shoulder, I noticed, he ushered us inside.

The interior of the cottage took me aback, for it was not what I expected to see. I cannot say for certain what it was that I did expect, but it was not that. One wall had been covered with makeshift shelves on which stood rows of dusty old books, sheaves of paper and a strange variety of stuffed animals. I saw a crow, two weasels and a rabbit and, most strange of all, on the top shelf was the skull of an animal that I could not identify. It was of a similar size to a sheep, but most definitely was not, for I had seen plenty of those in my time.

I had started to scan the books on the shelves and the mix was eclectic to say the least. But before I could look too deeply Stevenson had pulled down an old, leather-bound book with a brown cover, and had started flicking through the pages looking for something in particular. He found the page that he required and turned the book to face me.

'Was this roughly what you saw?' he asked me. On the page was a pencil drawing of a footprint of a remarkably similar size and shape to the one that I had found the previous night. I agreed that it was and he looked intrigued. He snapped the book shut before I had had time to study anything more of the handwritten notes which surrounded the image, save noticing that the top of the page had been labelled 'Yeth, to scale'.

I asked Stevenson what the book was, but he was not forthcoming with any information on its contents. But he did continue to inform me that it was part of a collection of items which he had acquired which originally came from a house called 'Brooke' which stood on the outskirts of Buckfastleigh, to the south of the county.

'The owner was a squire by the name of Richard Cabell,' Stevenson told me. 'He was something of a notorious character and, like me, he collected bizarre objects. A number of these things you see around you came from there. I came by them as a job lot and they are most interesting. A number of these books are most unusual and some have taken some work to decipher. I should not discuss their contents with you now, for I believe that there are things therein which are perhaps not suitable for Emily to understand just now.'

Emily looked downhearted, as she had been listening with avid interest – her child's mind no doubt racing with possibilities.

'Ah, but Emily wants to know more,' Stevenson chuckled. I started to protest but he stopped me in my tracks.

'Don't worry yourself, I shall say no more,' he continued. 'Emily, I shall show you and your brother something else instead. Something even more interesting and even more mysterious.' These last words he delivered to Emily in mock horror and her eyes widened.

He led us out through the parlour into his small garden, and down the path to a stone-built outhouse at the far end. Pushing open the door he drew us inside. Inside was a large piece of machinery, the likes of which I had never seen before. At the centre was what looked like a large copper boiler, with some kind of thick glass window, oval in shape, in its centre. Thick rivets held the glass in place and, behind it heavy steam or vapour seemed to circulate, although no heat radiated from the device. Metal pipes snaked from this chamber to smaller receptacles to the sides and, from the top, a large funnel disappeared through the roof of the outhouse.

Emily stared, as did I, at the machinery. It resembled nothing I had seen on any farm, or in any factory.

'What is it?' she asked Stevenson.

'Ah, now that is a good question,' he replied. 'What is it indeed. I'll tell you what it is, young Emily. It is a mystery, that's what it is. I have spent years trying to figure it out.'

Stevenson explained to us that the machinery had also come from Brooke, with the other ephemera, and had evidently also belonged to Squire Cabell. But its purpose continued to be a mystery. He had assembled it with the aid of diagrams which he had found in one of the books, but as to its purpose, he could not tell us. Or would not tell us, for I got the feeling that, although he professed no knowledge, he was concealing something. Why would he have brought us here otherwise, if not to show me the drawing of the footprint in the book?

I started to feel somewhat uncomfortable and decided that I should make my excuses for us to leave. I told him that I had wanted to pay a visit upon my beloved Cassandra, but that it was getting late and Emily needed to be taken back to the cottage for the evening duties. And so it was that we left Stevenson, and his books and his strange outhouse and walked back up through the old town to our home.

I delivered Emily back to the house and decided that I needed some time to think. Telling her to go and do her chores and to speak nothing of our afternoon to our parents (a request which I knew would be carried out for she was a good girl and would cause no trouble) I decided to take an evening constitutional.

My second experience of the Dog was that evening, during my walk. I had taken a circular route around the town, which was quiet and peaceful in the dimpsey light of dusk-time. I had probably strolled for three-quarters of an hour or so and was making my way back to the cottage along a back road, which was lined with trees and lit by the occasional gaslight which the lamplighter had fuelled probably half an hour previous.

The air and the countryside seemed strangely still. It struck me as odd, as the night birds, preparing to nest down for the evening, were usually still fluttering and twittering at this time. I thought on it as I walked and, inclining my head, listened more intently to the sounds of the countryside. Or rather, the quiet of the night, for I could still hear nothing.

After another minute or two, having slowed my pace somewhat to concentrate, I became aware of muffled footsteps in time with my own. I stopped, and immediately they ceased. I listened hard, but there was nothing and so I took a few tentative steps forward. They were there again, matching my pace but keeping the same quiet volume which suggested to me that they were never gaining nor losing distance. I stopped again and slowly turned. And there it was.

Standing on the edge of the pool of flickering light being cast downward by the gas lamp, I could make out an indistinct black mass. It seemed shapeless but, gradually, I became aware of two red marks cutting through the gloom – pinpricks at first, but the more I looked, the larger they became until they resembled two glowing coals hovering in the darkness. I stared at them, transfixed. I wanted to turn away, but I could not. Those glowing red orbs seemed to draw me in, to reach out and grab me by the very soul and pull me toward them, though physically my feet stayed planted to the spot and I did not move.

As I looked, the black cloud seemed to draw itself together into a form, melding out of the chaos to become more real, more solid, more animalistic. It drew forward slightly into the edge of the gas light glow and I could just make out the contours of the face in the shadows. Surrounding those two horrible eyes, as I now saw them to be, cheek and jowl materialised and an awful canine demeanour. As it solidified in my gaze I made out the body of the great Dog as it sat, stock still, on the edge of the light.

As I watched, it stared back. It did not move. It did not make a sound. It just stared. I wanted to turn away, to run in the other direction, but I could not. Those two great eyes just seemed to hold me in place. And then, as quickly as the apparition had formed it rose, backed away from me out of the light and was gone.

It took me probably fifteen or twenty seconds to gather my composure, although those seconds felt like minutes in their passing. When I could finally move, I turned tail and ran up the road as fast as I was physically able and back to the cottage. Bursting through the front door, I took the stairs two at a time to the top landing, into my room and shut and bolted the door fast. Despite the protestations of my family that I had not taken dinner, I refused to emerge for the rest of the night, giving no reason, until finally they gave up and left me in there. It was the last that I would hear of one of them.

I was awoken from a deep yet troubled sleep in the early light of dawn by the shrill scream of my mother from down below. I sat bolt upright, for there was sheer terror in the sound that emanated from beneath me. Throwing on my gown, I dashed from the room and was immediately confronted by the vision of a crumpled heap at the foot of the stairs. It was my father who, it had seemed, had tripped on a ruck in the rug on the landing and, losing his balance, had fallen to the floor below.

Emily ran from her room to see what the commotion was, but before she could get there I scooped her up and turned her away, for I could not let her see our father, lying dead before us with his neck snapped outwards at a sickening angle. I returned her to her room and held her tightly, sobbing with her as the screaming continued from the hall.....

He was buried three days later at the Church of St Michael in a simple ceremony, and in a simple grave. Of the intervening period I cannot speak, for it is too full of heartache and grieving for me. The church was full of local farmers and trades people, with which our family have always had a good relationship and we sat at the front in sombre silence, clad in traditional black, before following the coffin to the bleak graveyard outside, dampened by the common drizzle of the moor.

As we left the churchyard, Stevenson took me to one side extending his sympathies for our loss. Emily stopped with me, but our mother pulled her on and bade her return home. I left them to their slow walk and followed Stevenson, who requested that I walk down to his home for some refreshment and some time to talk. Feeling the need for a change of scenery I accepted his offer and we walked the short distance to his door in silence.

Once inside his strange cottage, he offered to brew some tea but, upon my request for something a little stronger under the circumstances, fetched two glasses of brandy from an archaic sideboard buried underneath piles of paper. We sat in two moth-eaten old armchairs for a couple of minutes, sipping the warming liquid, before Stevenson broke the silence.

'You've seen it again haven't you?' he enquired.

I stared at him, saying nothing, but my face must have told him the complete story where my words did not.

'Yes, you have,' he said. 'I knew it. And that is the cause. That is the fiend that is fairly responsible for the death of your father.'

I looked at him aghast, protesting that he had but tripped and fallen down the stairs, but Stevenson would have none of it.

'It is the Yeth hound,' he explained. 'It is a portent and you have looked into its eyes.'

I said nothing.

'Look,' he continued. 'You recall my telling you that Richard Cabell owned much of these things?' He gestured around him to the books and papers that lay strewn around the room. 'He knew of it, and he studied it. Of that I am certain. The legend is well known, but I believe now that it is more than a legend. There are references, paragraphs among these papers that refer to the animal in detail. I showed you the drawing of the footprint, the one that matched what you saw outside your window. There is more. It tells how anyone looking into the face of the beast is sure to suffer some death or disaster soon afterwards.'

I looked aghast and told him that he was being ridiculous; that he should have more care and consideration for what I had just been through. Draining my glass I rose to leave, but he grabbed my arm and pulled me back down into my chair.

'Calm yourself my friend,' he said gently. 'It is not ridiculous. It is all recorded here in these pages.' He waved his arm around the room in a wide sweep. 'Do you know how he died? He was, it is said - and I have no reason to doubt it under the circumstances - chased across the moor by a pack of demonic hounds. Run down by them. Hunted, if you will. Traditions say that he was an evil man and I believe that he had found some link, some bridge between here and somewhere else.'

I could not quite comprehend what he was telling me. Was he saying that the hounds had been 'summoned' in some way? It was not possible. I thought him mad to consider it, but then I thought on what I had already seen and experienced and wondered if maybe I was the one who was deranged. What had I seen those three days previous? Was it a trick of the light, or something more?

I came back to the present as Stevenson beckoned me up out of the chair to accompany him out into the garden. 'You look like you could do some with some fresh air,' he said. He recharged my glass and I followed him out onto the small lawned area to the rear of the property.

A small plume of black smoke rose from the makeshift chimney atop his old outhouse at the bottom of the garden. I remembered my previous visit and that strange contraption contained therein. Walking down the path I approached the grimy window of the outhouse and peered through the glass. There inside was that same large copper cylinder with its array of pipework. I gazed in at the oval viewing panel in the centre of it, wondering just what it was that was assembled in there.

The same wispy clouds of vapour rolled and circulated around the inside of the cylinder, but somehow they seemed darker than before. I watched them transfixed for a couple of minutes as they performed their strange, hypnotic dance before Stevenson called me back.

'Come on,' he beckoned, 'you should really get back to your mother and sister. I have kept you here long enough. I'll walk up the road with you. You could do with the company, I'm sure.'

I turned away from the window to join him at the top of the garden and, as I did so, I could swear that I saw two small glimmers of red among the swirling clouds.

My third experience of the Dog was but two weeks later ... and its tragedy was sadly no less than the previous. I was returning from a long day in the fields, where I had been tending to the flocks in readiness for the forthcoming sales. It was late at night by the time that I had finished and I came down across the fields as a mist was beginning to descend. The route was familiar to me, but it was easy to become lost in these wild landscapes when the fogs descended and so I had lit a storm lantern to keep my way true until I reached the edge of the town.

And here it was that I saw the infernal creature again. I had rounded the corner into the lane which wound towards our cottage when a bulk seemed to rise from nowhere out of the gloom ahead. The night was brisk, but not cold and yet I shuddered even as I saw the shape begin to form. This was not the shivering of inclemency, but rather that of a cold from within, as if the very blood in my veins were changing to ice water.

I knew at once what I was seeing and the voice of Stevenson echoed in my head from our earlier talk. The Yeth Hound. Could it possibly be so? Was Stevenson right? Did the creatures truly exist? I wondered if there was, indeed, some connection to the old tome which we had examined in Tavistock, to the ephemera of Squire Cabell which Stevenson told me of in his cottage. And what of the strange device in the outhouse?

Thinking back, it seems like so many questions and thoughts, but they raced through my mind almost as one before the creature had formed in front of me. It must have been mere seconds. Or maybe it was longer. My recollection of the events seems somehow hazy and distant now. I try to remember the details but I cannot. I know that I felt a sense of intense urgency. That I had to get past, to get home to the cottage. I sensed an impending doom, danger even, but I know now exactly what it was.

Once again, I could not move. I was transfixed, wanting to flee but being unable. And then, I remember ... what? It seems too odd, too curious to be right. I am sure that I remember that the Dog shape began somehow to transform as it solidified. But how? It does not seem possible, though I am convinced that somehow the head began to morph, to elongate and compress. Try as I might, I cannot bring the full detail of this horror to the forefront of my consciousness. Maybe the mental block is my own, maybe somehow it is from elsewhere. I would swear upon a dozen bibles that the features, the very visage of the creature became more .... human? And within that strange human/canine hybrid, if that recollection is even correct, I am sure that there was some form of familiarity.

I remember no more. Not until I became aware that I was running up to the cottage door. I burst through, not having looked behind me. The cottage was lit, which was as well as I no longer had the storm lantern. I know not where it went. I ran straight into the arms of Emily who was sobbing.

'Mother,' she cried, 'Mother.' She said nothing else. She could not. She just kept repeating the word over and over. I held her, trying to calm the hysteria and asked her where. She gestured to the garden but could say nothing more. I passed through the kitchen and out of the back door. There, in the gloom of the night I could see the crumpled body of our mother lying amongst a pile of shattered glass. I looked for the source of the mess, finding eventually that it had come from an upstairs window. She had obviously fallen through somehow, hitting the ground with a terrific shock that looked to have shattered her skull.

I turned away. There was nothing that could be done for her and my only thought now was for Emily. I went back to the kitchen and grabbed a bottle of brandy, the lone bottle that was kept for visitors or special occasions and poured two large helpings of the brown liquid into a couple of table glasses. I drank one draught, the other I took to Emily. Forcing her into a chair I made her drink it, trying anything in an effort to calm her.

She coughed and spluttered as the liquid went down her throat, her young palate being unfamiliar with hard liquor. But in a minute or two the alcohol had the desired effect and she began to calm slightly. I shook her, bringing her round and asked her what happened.

'She heard summat,' Emily spluttered between gasps from both the effect of the brandy and shortness of breath from crying. 'Somethin' hideous. T'was like a terrible howling from the fields. She thought summat was out there, after the sheep p'raps. She ran upstairs. I think she wanted to get a better look at 'en from the upstairs window.'

She paused for breath after having found enough voice to rattle out these happenings, before continuing.

'I heard a terr'ble scream. She was shoutin' at summat out of the window. Telling it t'go away. And then t'was a crash ... and then silence.'

I stared at her. I could not comprehend what was happening. This must have happened at the exact same time that I had whatever experience it was that I had undergone in the town. Was it truly the case that some creature, or was it now creatures, from the darkness were seeking me out somehow? At that moment I became convinced that everyone was in danger.

No. Not everyone. Everyone I knew. Everyone who was close to me. Father, dead. Mother, dead. I yelled at Emily that we had to leave, immediately. I knew not where, nor why, but we had to go. I dragged her from the chair, threw a coat around her and pulled her from the cottage, urging her to the paddock at the side where we kept our horse tethered.

We were both expert riders – everyone who worked the land was – and had no need of saddle or tackle to ride safely. Besides, there was no time for such things. I remained convinced we had to leave. I shouted at Emily to get on the horse and I clambered up behind her. Grasping her round the waist I drove a boot heel into the poor animal's flank and struck out for the moor, the horse being forced to vault the low stone wall before it knew what was happening.

We galloped at full speed across the fields and towards the open moorland, the dark crags of distant tors lit by the full moon now high in the sky above us. I had no idea where I was heading, nor did I care. I just knew I had to get Emily away from there.

It was then that it hit me. What of Cassandra? She was the only other person dear to me. Was I fleeing with one to leave another behind? Before I knew what I was doing I was turning the horse to ride back the other way. I had no plan in mind. I was working on instinct, but I knew that something was coming and that I alone could provide salvation for those around me.

And then it happened. We galloped headlong for a small copse and as we did so a huge black mass rose up from the trees in front of us and a terrific howl, as if the sky had opened and all of the demons of, I know not where, were shrieking from some lost realm. The horse started, turned and reared. Emily and I were thrown like two helpless rag dolls into the air. I hit the ground with a resounding crack...

... blackness ...

... silence ...

I suddenly became aware of a sound, as of steam escaping under pressure from a cracked pipe. A hissing, interspersed with some other strange noises started to play on the fringes of my hearing. Water. Or some other liquid moving. I could not see anything, but the sounds began to resolve. Metal on metal. Some form of grinding or clanking noise.

A light mist started to form on the edges of the blackness. I was sure that my eyes were closed still and yet I could see swirling patterns emerging from the dark. The noises grew louder in my ears and I started to become aware of shapes; long thin tube-like structures played across my vision, red flashes and turning circles. Everything was indistinct. But the noise grew ever louder. Hissing. Rushing. Snarling. Howling ....

My eyes flicked open. The light was blinding so I snapped them closed again, then opened them more slowly. The surroundings were unfamiliar. Brick walls. Whitewash. Floor tiles. As I came to my senses I realised that there were beds. And people.

'You're awake.' I heard a voice. Everything hurt but I slowly turned my head to the side, to see the face of Stevenson looking back at me. I looked confused and opened my mouth to ask a hundred questions.

'Not now,' he said. 'There can be a time for questions, but this is not it. I know you will have one in particular, and I am sorry to say that the answer to that one is no.'

He had, naturally, predicted that I would ask about poor Emily.

'You must rest,' he said. 'Drink this.' He offered me a glass and I took a small sip.

'More,' he insisted, 'you need more.' I struggled, but swallowed more of the clear liquid.

He told me to close my eyes, but even as he said it I could feel the lids starting to droop once again.

'I will return,' he said in a low voice. 'Later. In the meantime do not worry about anything, or anyone.'

I heard him walk away as I lay there. I felt weak, and tired, but somehow something was telling me that I could not rest.

As I lay in the dark, my mind returned to those images and sounds which I had heard before I had awoken. I struggled to bring them back to my memory. They reminded me of something familiar. What was it? The steam and the noise were certainly not unknown. And then it hit me. Stevenson's outhouse. The machinery.

The sounds and images faded and were replaced with one, bright and clear as day. Cassandra. It was at this moment that I realised that she must be in mortal peril. Everyone else close to me had gone. I had to save her. But how? And with that I fell into a deep sleep again.

I experienced the strangest dream. At least I believe it was a dream. Or could it have been a vision? A state of some unconscious wakefulness. I became aware of the room around me. And in the corner of the room sat a large black hound, staring at me with its deep red eyes. It cocked its head but, somehow, now I was not afraid. I rose from my bed and approached it and as I did so, it turned its back and walked from the room.

I followed it as it led me down corridors and stairs. We headed down to the lower level of the hospital, the Dog never looking back and keeping a constant distance in front of me. But I was compelled to follow. Eventually we reached what was obviously the cellar of the building. A large wooden door stood between us and the room beyond.

Suddenly, the Dog began to dissipate in front of me. It became a black mist of vapour, which seeped between the slats of the door, around the frame and underneath into the room beyond. I approached the door, holding out a hand to push it open.

Suddenly from within I heard a voice call my name. Loudly and with urgency. Cassandra...

... I awoke. I was lying in the bed as before, but somehow everything had suddenly become clear. Cassandra was in danger. She was the last person who was close to me, closer arguably than my family had been. And the Dog would take her as well. Unless...

... unless it took me first. I knew what I had to do. The only way to stop the Dog from taking Cassandra was to allow it to take me. I would have to kill myself that she may live. This was the meaning of the dream. I needed to go to the cellar. The answer - and the means of inevitable destruction - lay that way.

It was late, I calculated, and the building seemed to be sleeping. Many of the beds were empty and those that were not had curtains drawn around them. Being night, there were few staff around and they would be busy with their duties, likely to come only if summoned by the ringing of a patient's bell.

I rose painfully but with determination and headed from the dormitory room. There was no reason to pause, nothing to turn for. The corridors were exactly as they had appeared in my dream. I saw the turn of the corner and the stairs beyond, which I descended with purpose.

Suddenly, in front of me was the wooden door. It seemed warmer down here, hot almost. I pushed the door open and entered the cellar. The room was darker than the corridors down which I had headed, but lit with some form of strange orange glow.

The imagery of my previous visions came flooding back to my senses. I heard hissing, liquid, steam. In front of me stood a large metal structure – a machine – with pipework, levers, handles. A large metal cylinder stood at the heart with an oval glass panel riveted to the front like a viewing window. I was transported back to Stevenson's outhouse. This seemed reminiscent, almost identical in fact, though on a much larger scale.

So the hospital was some form of portal, or boundary. I approached the machinery and looked into the glass. The same swirling mist that I had seen at Stevenson's tumbled and fell within this device. Every so often, as it passed the glass, it seemed to form itself into recognisable shapes. An ear. A tail. A great paw. Without warning a great light erupted from the centre of the mist and a piercing red eye seemed to stare at me from within the bowels of the cylinder.

I knew what I had to do. In order to save Cassandra I would need to give myself to the Dog; cross the liminal perimeter into this other dimension so that she may live on. I looked to the pipes on the side of the machine, and the large metal valves and handles.

Reaching out, I wrapped my fingers around two large levers on the edge of the cylinder. The whole contraption seemed to vibrate and shudder, the steam hissing and whooshing past my head. The mist behind the glass seemed to become thicker and darker and great jaws appeared out of it gnashing and snarling.

My grip tightened and I closed my eyes as, slowly, my hands seemed to fuse themselves to the metal and I started to become part of the infernal device .....

The next two stories carry an
advisory 18 rating

Cutty Dyer
By P.J.Reed

William Crossing closed his battered laptop and smiled. Then fished his mobile from his green tweed jacket pocket and punched in the number of the lead and only writer of the Ashdurton Flyer. An almost monthly newsletter, its page filled with the excitement and intrigue found in most small Devon towns. Last month, its headline screamed a warning to all that a shed outbuilding had been broken into and a circular saw taken by two rough-looking men, who had previously knocked on Farmer Whyte's farmhouse door, looking for work. It had created such a wave of panic that the town's two part-time constables had been ordered to increase police presence in Ashdurton. They had achieved this request by eating their packed lunches on the outside picnic tables of the Shady Hound, the oldest public house in the ancient town.

'Hello Jack, is that you?' he asked.

The line crackled and wheezed as it slowly connected to Jack's ancient Nokia, which looked more like an army walkie-talkie, than a domesticated mobile.

'Aye! 'Tis!' Jack yelled down the phone, so loudly that if William had opened his front door, he would have heard Jack's voice from the open window of the silent pub sitting opposite his house.

'It's done. I just got the email through,' William shouted into the phone. 'We are going to be listed in *Dartmoor Noire*, the moorland directory of hauntings and magical places!'

'Oh aye! that's grand but there's no need to shout. I ain't dead yet you know,' Jack shouted back. 'Well then, come over yere an' read it to us. This deserves a proper celebration,' the voice decided, and the phone call ended.

William tutted and printed off the email, which he carefully folded up, and put in his leather briefcase, in case it became creased or was blown away by a sudden gust of wind howling down from the moor.

He paused for a moment by the rose-covered front door, checking his reflection in the hall mirror. William straightened his navy blue bow tie and patted down his greying hair. While the locals did not seem to care about their appearance or smell for that matter, William had been transplanted from the local government offices of the London Borough of Brumley. People from Brumley cared about their appearance above most things and he refused to let the decidedly lower standards of the south-west affect his standard of grooming.

William had decided to dedicate his newly found redundant freedom to using all his experience in local town planning application processing, into reinvigorating the depressed Devon town, with little character or sites of interest, into a must-see tourist destination.

The idea had come to him while watching a documentary on Netflix regarding dark tourism. Apparently, tourists paid an absolute fortune to be irradiated on trips around the dormant husk of the Chernobyl power station. William had done his research. The internet was swamped in selfies of vain young things posing outside vacant apartments, shops, and in the empty playground, which was now completely overrun with bushes, trees, and wildflowers. A child's swing moved in a slow metronomic beat in the abandoned playground pushed by the ash-filled winds as they played a lament for the dead and still dying. While all the time being watched by the concrete jacketed monster of the half-melted nuclear reactor. A distant deadly menace that had murdered thousands. It was a case of self-generating media promotion. Once the tourists arrived and started taking their inane selfies the site would sell itself William thought happily.

At first glance, Ashdurton did not seem very similar to Chernobyl.

The town lay on the sloping borders of the brooding beauty of Dartmoor National park, a dark shadow lurking just above the town's rooftops. William had tried to develop Ashdurton as an outward bound steppingstone onto the moor. He had had visions of jeep safaris, quad biking adventures, and even a horse riding centre. Unfortunately, both the moor and the town were covered by strict non-planning regulations and run by local bureaucrats who had no understanding of big commerce and only wanted to preserve the real estate untouched for future generations. Furthermore, they refused to even consider financing his vision.

It was a very short-sighted view but had led him to pursue other options, and onto the potential gold mine of the dark tourist.

He strode across the road and opened the sticky wooden door of the Shady Hound. It was filled with five locals all dressed in shades of 'countryside in winter,' sitting along a narrow, wooden bar.

'If I catch 'ee smoking again Noah, I'll 'ave to call 'ees mother. Mary will kill me if I don't,' the publican leaned over the bar as he polished a pint glass with a grey, tattered tea towel.

'Aw, but George I'm twenty-five now. I'm me own man,' the youth at the bar whined over his pint.

'Aye, but you still live at your ma's farm You treat your ma with respect boy,' a grim-faced, black-haired man in a dirty green flat cap muttered.

Noah bit his lip and fiddled with the frayed ends of the cuffs of his overlarge checked shirt.

William rolled his eyes.

'Hello everyone, has Jack told you all the great news?' William asked.

Five heads shook in unison. William glared over at Jack who was drinking on a private table by the empty stone fireplace.

'So you's buggering off back up to London then?' Noah grinned.

The rest of the bar dissolved into laughter.

'No, I'm not, thank you, Noah,' William said smiling as he pretended to enjoy the country wit. 'Ashdurton is going to be listed in the *Dartmoor Noire* guide. We are going to become an exclusive tourist destination.'

George the innkeeper scratched the side of his face with the glass he was wiping. While the grim-faced man's light grey eyes narrowed suspiciously.

'An' why do we want more foreigners yere then?' the man snarled.

'Now then, Crowie let 'im speak,' the barmen said casting a quick glance at Jack, who shrugged his broad shoulders and carried on drinking.

'Tourists bring in money. Ashdurton needs money. It's as simple as that,' William replied, 'and this is the way to do it. Just listen to this email regarding our proposed entry.'

Crowie stared into his pint glass, but Noah and the others looked up listening intently.

Satisfied he had an audience, William put his briefcase on the bar, pulled out the piece of paper and cleared his throat. 'The beautiful Devonian countryside with its wild moorland, ancient stone circles, and dark woodlands have always been special, surrounded by whispered tales of magic and myth. Some of these tales tell of good, helpful spirits, while others warn of supernatural creatures hungry for their human prey.

The town of Ashdurton lies to the south of Dartmoor in the heart of the South Devon countryside. Ashdurton is an ancient tin-mining town which dates to Saxon times. Over time, the town has spread along the path of the river Ashdurn. It is Ashdurton's relationship with this river that caused it to encounter a murderous supernatural entity that goes by the name of Cutty Dyer.

A thousand years ago Cutty made his home by the river, waiting hungrily beneath the King's bridge for prey. Sometimes he catches fish or pets out wandering by themselves. Other times, he fancies larger prey. Over the past millennia, there have been documented cases of villagers, particularly, drunk men going missing on their way home crossing over the river Ashdurn. The *Dartmoor Noire* bus tour will visit Ashdurton for a one hour stop as part of its monthly, 'Ride The Beast Tours.'

William looked up peering over the sheet of paper.

The smile faded from his flushed face as five blank faces stared back at him.

'So, you're sayin' all this fuss is fer a bunch of tourists bussed in to see our bridge fer an hour every month?' Farmer Whyte took off his green woolly cap which cunningly covered most of his bald pate. His hairline restricted to a narrow ribbon of cropped grey which circumnavigated his head.

'What? Are they are goin' to stand an' watch the river fer an hour, that don't sound like a good outing, just how much are they payin'? They could come an' watch my stream fer a tenner if they wanted to,' Whytie stated and winked at Jack.

Noah roared with laughter, snorting into his beer. The golden liquid flew everywhere. George flapped his tea towel at

Noah and yelled, 'Bloody well clean yer own mess up, young 'un.'

'One hour don't seem much do it?' George stared intently at William. 'Why can't they stay fer longer an' have a traditional Devonshire cream tea or ploughman's lunch. Young Amberley could do either?'

William breathed heavily.

Carefully, he folded the paper into a quarter rectangle and put it into the plastic envelope which he placed into his briefcase. Then snapped the locks shut and looked at the giggling locals with thinly veiled disappointment.

'We are very lucky to get them to stop in this shitty little backwater at all. If it weren't for the three missing dogs from Hope Farm, which I convinced them were taken by Cutty, the tour wouldn't be bloody well stopping here at all. The tour guides will be making their preliminary visit tomorrow.' He grabbed his briefcase and marched from the pub.

'Well, there be no need for that sort of language,' Jack said shaking his head. 'Bloody grockel, if he don't like it yere why don't 'ee just bugger off back to London an' take all his fancy plans with him.' He stared philosophically into the murky bits floating in the bottom of his glass of real ale.

'What we need is a bigger draw, three dead dogs 'tis nothin',' the innkeeper moaned as he picked up Whytie's dirty glass and took them back to Amberly in the kitchen.

'But how'd 'ee know the dogs was dead, Crowie?' Noah asked as he nervously chewed on his black rimmed fingernails and turned towards the silent, black-haired farmer.

'Some things are best not asked, boy,' the farmer growled and stood up. Then followed William from the pub.

The innkeeper picked up the last dirty pint glass and wiped over the bar scrubbing away the sticky patch where Noah had spilt his ale. His face hurt from smiling. It was one of the many disadvantages of his job that, and the gradually decreasing debt mountain he had inherited from his father when the old man disappeared almost three years ago. Since that time even if the pub did not make a profit every month at least it was not haemorrhaging money anymore. He was a far superior businessman than anyone in the village. He had got rid of the cleaner and that expensively trained, loudmouthed Janner-chef shipped in from Plymouth. It was just him and the girl Amberley now. Amberley was a good employee. She worked for less than minimum wage and was grateful too. More importantly, she didn't know one end of a cow from the other. As long as the meat was minced, she cooked it, no questions asked.

The innkeeper quickly rinsed the dirty pint glass and put it back underneath the bar. One of his economies had been to sell the dishwasher. It had just sat in the corner of the kitchen guzzling his water and electricity. It was literally money down the drain. To be honest, even with a quick splash of water, his crockery and glassware were still a lot cleaner than most of his customers he mused. George took his shotgun from the shelf below the glasses and switched the remaining lights off.

He locked the pub door and vanished into the darkness.

William watched the pub lights die, checked his watch, and tutted. It was 10.30pm, the pub was supposed to shut at 11 pm. George Smallbrook was clocking off early yet again.

He sighed.

It was so hard being the only reliable businessman in the town, but he had a mission to complete. William had promised his mother, on her death bed, that he would be a success and finally make her proud of her son. He could feel her looking down from heaven watching over him still. The *Dartmoor Noire* tour would be his greatest achievement. He reached over to the white bedside table, picked up a large silver photo frame, and kissed the photo of a severe-looking woman with grey hair carefully curled around her head as she stared intently into the camera.

'Goodnight mother,' William whispered, as he replaced the photo frame on the table.

William snuggled down into the bed, lying on his left side as he stared at the photo. His attention was drawn to the wrinkled white wallpaper. Its ends were peeling away from the top of the wall. Dried watermarks trickled down from the corners of the wall leaving light brown trails.

The wallpaper by the double-hung Victorian windowsill was particularly stained. The window must have been left unlatched during a winter storm he reasoned. The wallpaper beneath the windowsill hung in brown tatters. The plaster peering from the ripped paper was ringed with concentric brown circles and smelt of wet earth. While to the left of the window frame, was the light brown impression of his mother's handprint.

It was strange, as he did not remember her hand being so large.

His mother would have hated the state of her room and chastised him severely for letting the house get so dusty. In his adult years, he had begun to enjoy her punishments and she had banished him. It had been her final chastisement.

Now, the room looked more like a tomb than a bedroom, but he did not have the heart to touch anything. William wanted it left exactly the way it was – the last time she slept here.

He turned off the white china lamp and closed his eyes. His fingers felt the small embroidered flowers on the duvet. The wrinkled white bedsheet stuck to the small of his back. William knew he should change the bedding, but it still held traces of mother's musk.

He smiled happily and soon fell fast asleep.

William woke the next morning to the sound of swearing coming from beneath the window as Farmer Whyte wheeled a barrow of fresh farm vegetables along the street, heading towards the King's bridge.

William opened the window and yelled down, 'For God's sake. What are you doing?'

'I'm taking my best veggies to the bridge. Them's city folk pay a fortune for organic veg. I heard it straight from old man Littlejohn at the last Farmers Market in Exhaven,' Whytie's faded hazel eyes glinted cunningly.

'But they are not coming today!' William shouted down. He clenched both fists, his fingernails digging red crescents into his palms. 'Only the tour guides will be here today, to examine the local area for signs of paranormal activity and write their talks.' He glared at Whyte. 'And what they don't want to see is a load of bloody vegetables!'

'Aye... but they gots to eat somethin' don't they?' Whytie grinned as he trundled off down the narrow road.

William swore.

Then he spun around in horror to face his mother's photograph. He could tell by her fixed black stare that she was angry. Quickly, he muttered an apology and threw on his clothes. A touch of mildew had made them feel slightly clammy against his skin and tinged with the smell of damp earth, but he doubted anyone would notice. Besides which, he had to get to the bridge before the local's lined it with so much tat the paranormal tour guides could not even see the river.

William scurried to the kitchen, made himself a cup of coffee and several slices of toast, smothered in sticky orange marmalade, which dribbled down his chin. He wiped it off with the back of his hand and raced through the front door. Then stopped dead in his tracks.

On the porch steps were two overlarge wet footprints, that seemed to appear from nowhere. The rest of the little front garden path was footprint clear.

'Bloody yokels,' he muttered to himself.

He had almost become accustomed to their little practical jokes over the past few months. The worst being the two dead rooks laid out by his back door, the bunches of stinking mugwort tied to his door knocker, and a sackful of decomposing rats. He had hoped that by ignoring their pathetic pranks they, whoever they were, would grow bored and cease their torments. Unfortunately, the pranks had been getting closer together and more disgusting as each week passed. After the tour guides, he would have to take a more proactive stance and report his harassment to the police. He was sure the silently brooding Crowie was behind it all or perhaps young Noah or anyone in the little town for that matter.

William paused for a moment as the lavender bushes lining the path swayed in the gentle breeze and the air filled with the heady scent of heating lavender. He took a deep breath, banished Crowie's face from his thoughts, and scurried down the purple-lined path.

It was going to be a good day.

His heart sank when he turned the corner and saw the little bridge lined with a noisy crowd of villagers, which spilt over into the normally vacant market carpark.

'Well, shame on you George Smallbrook,' Mrs Brown's indomitable voice screeched above the noise. 'Noah didn't come 'ome last night an' it's all your fault. That pub of yours is nothin' but a den of vice an' debauchery. I will bring it up at the next council meeting, you see if I don't. Servin' minors an' all.'

'But Noah isn't a minor,' George growled scowling at the shrunken farmer's wife.

'He's a boy an' he'll be a boy 'til I tells 'im otherwise,' Mrs Brown glared back at the publican. 'An' don't think I don't know that you've been slippin' him ciggies. Shame on you!' she screamed and pushed her way through the villagers waiting to see the celebrities from *Dartmoor Noire*.

'Forget bloody Noah. Two of me ewes was stolen last night. I found wool an' blood trails leading down into the village. Gert big ewes them were too. Take someone mighty strong to drag they.' Farmer Ashby scratched his chin and sized William up and down. Shook his head and went back into the crowd to continue his search for a gert big lad covered in wool stuck down with brown blood.

While in the one-lane road leading up to the bridge, Arthur Whyte waggled two deformed turnips in front of some terrified looking but well-dressed young men with *Dartmoor Noire* emblazoned in white letters across matching black T-shirts.

William pushed his way towards the tour guides and proffered his hand apologizing profusely about the locals.

The taller guide took off black tinted sunglasses and mopped his forehead delicately with a crisp white handkerchief. A carrot rolled off Whytie's handcart and was snatched by Skillet, Reverend Anderson's lightning-quick Jack Russell who disappeared through the crowd, heading back to the sanctuary of the chapel with its ill-gotten gains followed by a torrent of expressive swearing.

'Can we just see the spot where Cutty was seen and then we will just go, thank you?' the smaller tour guard stated, glancing at his gold-faced wristwatch. William noticed he still used a wind-up watch with moving hands. It was probably part of his paranormal investigating kit. William squinted at the watch.

Unfortunately, the elegant gold hands were sweeping around the clock face in an annoyingly clockwise fashion.

'Would you like to sample the local inn food before we examine the bridge or go on a walk around and see the sights of Ashdurton,' William suggested waving his hand towards the imposing clocktower of St Lawrence Chapel.

The smaller man sighed dramatically and looked at his wristwatch for a second time.

'Sorry we would love to but I have an important video conference with America at noon, business you understand.'

William nodded in shared sympathy of the hectic life of the international businessman.

'Well then, Cutty normally only comes out at night to take drunkards trying to cross his bridge, but we can go under the bridge and look for signs of paranormal activity?' William suggested.

'Yes, please do,' said the taller guide who towered over his partner, standing with his hands on his hips, legs apart, dominating the space as he surveyed the Ashdurtonites with detached disdain. William caught him rolling his eyes at his companion who lifted one oiled blond eyebrow in return.

The smile froze on William's face.

Obviously, they did not realise just who they were talking to.

He had been the Planning Department 'Employee of the Month' in January 2017 and he still had the photograph in his wallet to prove it. William would have framed the picture if only Mrs Frazer, the Head of the Planning Department had not looked so scared as she tried to edge away from him. It was surprising that she had managed to obtain a senior position with such a severe degree of social anxiety. However, she did wear gaudy blue eyeshadow. He had found the little container complete with a tiny foam tipped brush when she had gone to a meeting and left her desk drawer unlocked. She must have slept with the spotty man in Human Resources to attain the promotion over him. Woman who painted themselves were little more than prostitutes. Mother had told him that.

On the edge of the crowd, William saw the dark green figure of John Crow standing with his cap pulled down over his gaunt face, his hunting dogs circling his boots.

'Well you had better follow me then,' he said curtly, glaring at the smaller *Noire* tour guide. 'But be warned, Cutty sometimes attacks stock too and displays his trophies. I do hope you two are not squeamish.'

The taller guide gave William a strange look that he could not understand and grunted a negative.

William doubted they believed him. He smiled to himself. They would be in for a shock. If they wanted proof of Cutty's existence, they would certainly get it and it would serve them right.

He scrambled down the weed-infested bank and walked next to the equally weed-infested stream, heading towards the ancient stone bridge.

A pungent wave of newly decaying flesh hit him, and he crossed his fingers hoping Crowie had not done something too weird with the sheep. He looked back at the crowd, but Crow was lost in a blur of faces. The smell grew worse as he approached the underside of the stone bridge. The two tour guides breezed past him and marched into the shadows.

'What the hell?' William heard the tall guide exclaim.

'This is just sick,' the other agreed.

William ran towards the shadows. 'Is there a problem?' he enquired innocently.

'You people are simply vile. How could you do that to the poor sheep? It's just sick and the ridiculous Halloween decoration is obviously a cheap fake. Is the realm of paranormal investigations just a joke to you? We at *Dartmoor Noire* take the paranormal very seriously. It's people like you who give our business a bad name. You are hereby banned from our tour, our website, and from listening to the *Dartmoor Lore* podcast... for life!'

The tour guides pushed passed William and marched angrily back to their van. The taller guide slammed the shiny black van doors shut and *Dartmoor Noire* revved away into the distance.

William felt rage flood through his veins. Images of his hands around Crowie's throat squeezing his neck until his face turned blue and his lifeless body dangled in his hands flashed through his mind.

He ran beneath the bridge and stopped dead.

Barely visible in the shadows cast by the bridge's arc were three shiny metal poles.

On the two opposite poles were the missing sheep's heads, their eyes cloudy grey as they seemed to hover in the darkness. On the middle pole was the grey Halloween head. It's eyes and mouth sewn tightly shut with big black cross stitches. It looked like a doll head from a horror B-movie on Netflix.

William ripped it off the pole and threw it against the inner brickwork of the bridge. It made a squelching sound and plopped onto the floor as a small halo of brown blood oozed from the broken head. Gingerly, William toed the head over onto its front with his boot and stared down at its now crushed features.

The shaking started in his hands and then welled up through his entire body.

He stumbled backwards falling bottom first into the murky grey water and sat there for a minute gasping for breath as he realised Noah was dead and he had just bounced his decapitated head against the bridge.

Mrs Anderson, the vicar's wife, who had followed them under the little bridge, dropped the tray containing three mugs of tea and some slices of carrot cake and screamed, 'He's playing football with Noah's head!'

A white-tipped wave rippled through the grey waters towards William.

William sat in the water in terror as he watched a man appear from beneath the waves. The man rose from the river, the water dripping from his muscle-bound torso. He had a mane of wild black hair and he spoke through razor-sharp teeth.

'Have you bought me more dinner?' The man pointed his finger at William its long black pointed nail touching the tip of William's nose. 'You're not Crow, are you seconds then?' Cutty lunged towards William.

William fell backwards into the river, rolled onto his front, and kicked at Cutty's face.

Cutty tried to grab a flailing leg but could see little in the dark with the sprays of grey water.

William felt adrenaline surge through his veins, leapt from the water and ran from the bridge screaming, 'Cutty Dyer is under the bridge. He almost killed me!'

He felt himself being hurled onto the ground as cold steel handcuffs clinked around his wrist. The police officers nodded at each other. It was lucky the viewing had been held on a Thursday when the Ashdurton police station was open. It had been the first crime in Ashdurton since poor Mrs Crow had gone missing last year.

The crowd watched in silence as William was escorted across the ridge and into the police car for the short journey to the station in Apple Street.

Mrs Brown came up to John Crow supported by two anxious-looking elderly ladies and hissed, 'Next time sacrifice one of your own, Crowie or I'll carve 'ees name beneath the bridge for Cutty.'

'We've all lost someone, Mary,' said the innkeeper grimly. 'Now go 'ome the lot of you,' he said to the hushed crowd. 'We didn't see nothin' yere.'

Bobbing
By Jenny Kane

Feeling like a malevolent Eve slithering through the Garden of Eden, Libby did a slow twirl in the centre of the old cider barn.

The gauze dress was thin. It caressed her skin with a teasing arousal.

She was fertility herself.

If Robert hadn't wanted her before, he'd definitely want her now. But if she was honest, that had never been a problem. Robert always wanted her. He always wanted everyone. And her boss usually got what he wanted.

The scrumpy's pungent presence accosted Libby's nostrils as she ascended the ladder propped against the eight foot high cider barrel. Empting a box worth of apples into the liquid, she watched as the fruit bobbed across the foamy alcoholic surface.

Smiling into the vat's depths, Libby counted the apples, making sure there were enough for all the guests to have a go at capturing one with their teeth. Then, balancing with care, she reached up to the ceiling. A stick hung horizontally from ropes above the barrel. Tying a beeswax candle to one end and an apple on string to the other, Libby gave the stick a gentle push. She watched in satisfaction as it swung back and forth over the barrel of Devonshire's best cider.

Returning to the ground, Libby checked the collection of silk ties next to the steps. Each one waited patiently, ready to remove the potential bobber's temptation to cheat, by fastening their hands behind their backs.

Libby experienced an unexpected flash of power as she heard the approach of Robert's distinctive footsteps. It was difficult not to grin when she remembered how pleased he'd been on suggesting that he should be the first to try out the ancient apple catching ritual.

Fingering her pentagram shaped pendant, Libby's mind filled with images of ancient Pagan fertility rites she'd seen in history books.

'You wanted a traditional Pagan celebration boss, and this is it. There's alcohol soaked bread to be offered to the trees in the orchard, cider ready to be poured onto roots to toast the tree's health, apple bobbing, and of course, the apple stick.'

Allowing Robert to slip his arms around her waist, Libby wasn't surprised when he shuffled close enough for her to feel his crotch against her butt. Rather than examine the beauty of the Celtic scene she'd created, Libby knew Robert would be checking to make sure no one else was in the barn.

He glided his hands from her waist to her chest. She let him. As the moment to execute her plan grew ever closer, Libby's body had been on the cusp of an increasing impatient sexual high.

Robert peered up at the hanging stick. 'It looks impossible! And dangerous.'

Easing from his grasp, Libby chuckled dismissively as she climbed the ladder and lit the end of the swinging candle. Her eyes flared with the fizz of the wick as it caught. 'Don't worry; it's the cool wax sort they use in S&M clubs for candle play.'

Sliding back down, pushing herself against Robert's body, Libby smiled as she watched what she'd said sink into his imagination.

He grinned. 'Is that so?'

'You wouldn't think your pretty little PA would know of such things would you?' Having been careful to make the celebration to appear as Sara's idea, Libby knew this was her chance to press the point home. 'She always comes across as so innocent.'

'Was that Sara's idea too?' Robert's smile gave him away as he gestured towards the swinging stick. 'Where is Sara anyway, shouldn't she be helping you?'

'Oh she'll bob up sooner or later.' Libby winked as she gestured to the ceiling. 'You could consider this a bout of hot foreplay.'

'It won't scorch me?'

'Think of it as being anointed with cool grease. A minor inconvenience compared with the rewards to follow.'

Robert's eyes sparkled, 'I had no idea you and Sara were into this fertility stuff. I'd have encouraged a Pagan celebration every month rather than once a decade if I'd known!'

As his hands worked their predictable way through Libby's skimpy layers, she revelled in Robert's gasp of surprise. He'd just discovered she wore no underwear beneath her outfit.

'Well, what did you expect me to wear to a fertility rite?'

'Will all the guests be so, ummm, undressed?'

Libby gave a playful chuckle. 'Even little miss PA if you're lucky.'

Robert's hands stilled. Libby could almost hear him wondering if she knew. He really was thick when it came to women. She held in a groan as he added, clearly as an afterthought to ensure he'd get his leg over, 'I bet she won't look as hot as you.'

No, she won't.

Twisting her to face him, Robert buffed Libby's taut nipples through her thin clothing. 'We've got time haven't we?'

While her boss manhandled her tender flesh, Libby relished the scent of beeswax from the flaming candles. It enhanced the forever aroma of apples that cloaked the barn.

Continuing to inhale and exhale the almost festive atmosphere, Libby began to wonder if her calculations concerning the time it would take for human skin to separate from the bone, were accurate.

Pulling off his shirt, Robert kicked Libby's legs open with his foot. 'Come on Lib, I need a fuck.'

Letting her body get on with benefitting from the urgent masculine attention, Libby's brain considered how long it might be before a corpse's natural gases drove something wedged at the bottom of a barrel of acidic liquid to rise to the surface.

Robert's cock knocked clumsily at her thigh. 'You're a wicked woman, wife of mine.'

'True.' Resting her head on her husband's shoulder, Libby counted his thrusts. Three more and he'd be done. Predictable to the last.

Digging painted fingernails into his shoulders, Libby luxuriated in Robert's wince of pain as she clawed her base gratification into his flesh. Taking this unprecedented marital ecstasy as a sign that the fertility goddess had blessed her enterprise, and overcome by an apple scented climax, Libby milked her husband harder.

Bolstered by the unexpected gift of actually enjoying sex with her husband, Libby faced what lay ahead with an enhanced inner rush of success. From now on she was going to take pleasure in everything.

With a squeeze of his shoulder, Libby whispered into his ear, 'We should hurry. The guests will be here soon. We should have a trial run of the apple stick catching.'

Taking advantage of Robert's lingering blissed out state, Libby picked up his wrists and secured them behind his back with a strip of silk before he noticed what she was doing. 'Up you go. All you have to do is grab the apple using your teeth, and try not to get splashed by the dripping wax.'

'Not to mention, stopping myself from falling into the drink!'

'You won't fall in. The only way to overbalance, even if the stick swings as far out as it can go, would be if someone pushed you. As I'll be watching all the time, no one else will get that chance.'

The wax of the hanging candle had begun to melt. She heard it spatter onto the apples bobbing in the vat. 'Go on!'

'Are you sure it's OK, Lib?' He frowned. 'I'm sure I heard a loud splash while we were busy, more like something heavy dropping in than wax.'

'You imagined it.' She crossed her fingers behind her back. 'Anyway, that's why we're here!' Libby pushed him up the steps. 'Health and safety say we have to do a test run before the guests arrive. Honestly, people have been playing this game in Devon and Somerset since Celtic times. It'll be fine!'

Perched on the top rung of the ladder, Robert's hips were jammed hard against the rim of the barrel. Libby giggled as his first attempt to grab the apple between his teeth led to the rope swaying faster, sending the wax dripping like a shower of rain into the barrel.

'Oh, you almost had it!' Libby applauded as Robert leant a fraction further forward. His neck strained towards the swinging apple, his eyes screwed into narrow slits so he didn't get wax in them.

Libby climbed up the ladder behind him, 'I may have to rethink the tethers. Silk is a bit slippery. It could undo, and people might cheat.' Taking a firm hold of her husband's trapped wrists with one hand; Libby danced her free fingertips over his groin.

Instantly, Robert's cock hardened. He was so easy to re-arouse it was pathetic.

'Oh, Lib, if you do that I'll...'

'You'll what darling?' Libby gripped his shaft through his jeans.

'Nice, that's...Fuck!' A splash of melted candle hit Robert's face. 'That was hot! Christ! I thought you said it wouldn't hurt?'

Whipping his head round, Robert glared at her; an angry burn blooming on his right cheek.

Maintaining her grasp of his wrists with both hands, Libby prevented her struggling husband from wiping the wax away. 'Christ Libby! It stings like hell, you said...'

'I've said a lot of things.' Libby smiled brightly. 'Sara said it hurt as well. With her being so small, I thought she'd manage to avoid getting burnt when she tested it earlier. That bit was supposed to have been just for you, in lieu of having your fingers burnt for being a multiple cheating shit.'

Panic and realisation hit Robert simultaneously, just as Libby blew a kiss towards his scalded skin and heaved him bodily upwards and forwards, into the giant barrel.

The vision of her adulterous husband's head hitting the lit candle, his hair flaming with intense heat as he crashed into the alcohol, would keep Libby warm for years.

Exalting in the sight of the spluttering figure trying, and failing, to break through the weight of the bobbing apples, Libby waved at his frightened face. 'Say hi to Sara.'

Even after Robert's head had disappeared, pleasing bubbles from his last breath popped up between the apples.

Once the only sound in the barn was the thump of her own pulse, Libby stripped off her thin outfit. Naked, she scooped the apples from the surface of the barrel, hung a thick rope over the side, and dived in after Robert.

The matching burns on their faces weren't visible in this new world of amber liquid, but Libby was satisfied that the wounds would speed up the rate of skin disintegration.

By the time the real Pagan celebration came round next month, it wouldn't just be apple skin floating on the surface. With luck, this would be their best scrumpy ever.

Meet the Authors

Maura Beckett

Maura Beckett was born in North Devon, in the early 1970s and has lived in many parts of the UK. However, her love of the South-West drew her back and she is now based in Tiverton. Maura was a primary school teacher for 15 years and is currently a stay-at-home mum, fitting in writing around three school-aged children.

Maura is a member of both Exeter Authors Association and Twyford Writers, based in Tiverton. Her first short story submission resulted in a third place at the Tiverton Literary Festival competition in 2016, which inspired her to expand her ambitions and write a full-length novel.

As a debut novelist, she is working through the final edits of her book, The Daneton Affair, due for publication in 2020. Set in North Devon, the story is a cosy mystery drawing on Maura's love of her childhood home and her experiences as a teacher. She is also plotting the follow up novel which will see the protagonist move to Normandy, France to solve an old family mystery dating back to World War Two, with her Aunt.

Away from writing, Maura has a Black Belt in the martial art of Aikido and enjoys running, which she could do with doing more often. She also loves reading and watching mysteries, particular favourites being Midsomer Murders and Poirot.

Contact Maura at:

www.maurabeckett.com

Twitter: @maurabeckett1

E-mail: maurabeckett1@gmail.com

Jenifer Braund

Jeni has been writing for most of her life, starting with stories to amuse her classmates and getting detentions for writing in the back of her maths exercise book. Those in this collection are much more recent.

Stories and poems have appeared in local magazines and newspapers. In her professional life as a nurse she wrote academically and has been published in a national journal. She has also written courses on death dying and bereavement for her work in the NHS, one of which became a degree module for professional nurses.

In 2016 Jeni published *Heartlands* her first book of poetry, available on Amazon. Proceeds from the book are donated to Anthony Nolan the Blood cancer charity. Jeni also gives talks to local organisations on her life in nursing (44years in the NHS) and on her poetry.

Jeni is married with 3 children and 7 grandchildren. A personal quest for truth grew through the Anglican Church into which she was confirmed at 19. Years later it was to delve deeply into the mystical approach of the major religions when she studied Psychology and Comparative Religion with the Open University. Nursing started in a London hospital when she was 17 and spanned some 40 years in the NHS with a period in private work as her family grew up. Like all nurses she saw much of death and healing. It became a specialist subject following a 6 week residential palliative care course at St Christopher's Hospice in Kent where she studied under Dame Cicely Saunders. It was here she found her professional teaching vocation leading to both clinical teaching and higher education; developing courses for professional nurses in Death Dying and Bereavement for adults, children and their families.

You can contact Jeni at jeniferbraund@googlemail.com .

Her website address is **Jenibraund.com** and has links to **@Anthony Nolan** the blood cancer charity

Richard Dee

I was never a writer, at least not for ages. I made up stories in my head, based on dreams and events in my life, but I never did much with them. Life, a wife, three daughters and now three grandchildren have kept me busy.

I spent forty years in shipping, firstly at sea, then in Port Control and as a Thames River Pilot, with adventures to match anything I could imagine. When I retired, I just moved them out into space, changed some of the names and wrote them down.

I write Science Fiction and Steampunk adventures, as well as chronicling the exploits of Andorra Pett, reluctant amateur detective.

When I'm not writing, I bake bread and biscuits, cook delicious meals and walk the Devon coast.

I've published twelve novels, as well as two collections of short stories. I'm currently working on more prequels, sequels, and a few new projects.

You can find me at www.richarddeescifi.co.uk

K.Y.Eden

K.Y. Eden (Kristina) lives in Exmoor in the South West of England. She loves being outdoors in nature and spends most of her spare time with her family, horses and dog. Before becoming a writer she worked as a lecturer in the creative industries teaching drama, performing and production arts.

Always having a love for the arts she attended drama school in childhood and later gained degrees in Theatre & Performance and Performance Production. Further post graduate study resulted in her specialising in creative writing - scriptwriting and teaching. Kristina is an eclectic writer, and enjoys reading and writing in a variety of genres and disciplines.

Author website – kyedenbooks.wixsite.com/mysite

Janet Few

Janet Few inhabits the past. You may find her lurking in her four hundred year old North Devon cottage, or spot her thinly disguised as the formidable Mistress Agnes. This alter ego is a goodwife of a certain age, who leads a somewhat chaotic life during the mid-seventeenth century. One way or another, most of Janet's time is spent working to inspire others with a love of history, heritage and the written word.

In a vain effort to support her incurable book buying habit, in the past, Janet has been known to pull the odd pint or two, sell hamsters and support very special schoolchildren. Somewhere along the way, she acquired a doctorate in community history 'for fun'. Janet has an international reputation as a family historian, giving presentations across the English-speaking world. She has written several non-fiction history books and has recently turned to fiction. Like *Brought to Book*, which is based on a true story, Janet's first novel *Barefoot on the Cobbles* was inspired by an historic incident. One hundred years ago, in the euphoria of the armistice, a young woman lay dying in a North Devon fishing village. Her parents were to stand trial for her manslaughter. After a century of secrecy, Janet's novel uncovered the true story of the troubled individuals involved and the traumas in their pasts that led to this tragedy. A second novel, set in the turbulence and intolerance of seventeenth century North Devon, is being carefully nurtured. For further details about Janet's writing see

https://thehistoryinterpreter.wordpress.com/barefoot-on-the-cobbles-a-devon-novel

Any time that Janet can carve from her history-obsessed existence, is spent embarrassing her descendants, travelling and trying to make her garden behave itself. Janet is fascinated by human behaviour, past and present, real and fictional. Her love of the wonderful Devon landscape shines through her writing.

J E Hall

J E Hall has recently produced a number of contemporary thrillers on the challenging threat posed by extremism and issues of our time. Set in London the Middle East, Turkey and Devon they are a great read. Though his novels are all linked, they can be read independently of each other. Accolades have come from Rowan Williams, Ann Widdecombe amongst others. His inspiration is drawn from his personal experiences travelling and meeting people at home and abroad.

A one time Academic, Probation Officer and Church of England minister, the characters he draws have depth and the stories he tells are gripping.

His books are Flashbacks (2016), IStanbul (2017), Harry's England (2017), Domain (2018) and Truth (2019) with more to come!

Jenny Kane

From the comfort of her café corner in Mid Devon, award winning author, Jenny Kane, has written 12 contemporary women's fiction and romance novels, including, *Romancing Robin Hood* (2nd edition, Littwitz Press, 2018), *Abi's Neighbour* (Accent Press, 2017), *Another Glass of Champagne* (Accent Press, 2016), and the bestsellers, *Abi's House* (Accent Press, June 2015), and *Another Cup of Coffee* (Accent Press, 2013).

Jenny is also the author of quirky children's picture books *There's a Cow in the Flat* (Hushpuppy, 2014) and *Ben's Biscuit Tin* (Hushpuppy, 2015)

As Kay Jaybee, Jenny has been writing erotica for the past 14 years, winning a number of awards, including ETO Best Erotica Writer. She has written over 200 erotic stories, long and short, including the bestselling, The Perfect Submissive trilogy. (www.kayjaybee.me.uk – OVER 18's ONLY)

As Jennifer Ash, Jenny has just completed her first novel and fourth audio-script for ITV's revival of the hit 1980s series, Robin of Sherwood. She has also written the medieval crime series, The Folville Chronicles (The Outlaw's Ransom, The Winter Outlaw, and Edward's Outlaw).

Jenny Kane is the writer in residence for Tiverton Costa in Devon. She also co-runs the creative writing business, *Imagine*. (www.imaginecreativewriting.co.uk)

All of Jennifer Ash's and Jenny Kane's news can be found at www.jennykane.co.uk

Twitter @JenAshHistory @JennyKaneAuthor

@Imagine_Writing

Imagine www.imaginecreativewriting.co.uk

Richard Lappas

With almost 40 years experience, Richard has worked for a wide range of clients, including corporate and PR, national newspapers and magazines, sport, fashion, the NHS and local government. In creating images for marketing, brochures or websites he's well used to handling tight deadlines, working to brief, advising on media formats and delivering within set budgets.

As a member of the National Association of Press Agencies and the British Association of Journalists, Richard is regularly commissioned for assignments right across the south west region. Hundreds of his photographs have been published around the world.

From his office at Tiverton, on the Devon-Somerset border, he also provides a wedding photography service - producing high-quality work at competitive prices. A good wedding photographer should be creating a piece of family history and Richard prides himself on 'telling the story of the day' in a discreet, thorough and professional manner.

You can find Richard at

http://www.richardlappasimages.com

Mark Norman

Mark Norman is a folklore author and researcher. He is the creator and host of The Folklore Podcast, a global internet podcast on folklore which enjoys a wide following. Mark's first book, 'Black Dog Folklore' was published by Troy Books in 2015 and remains the only full length study by a single author on the folklore associated with apparitions of ghostly black dogs. The content was based on Mark's archive of traditions and reports, which is the largest such collection in the UK. Mark has written for a number of magazines and websites, has a regular column on folklore in The Moorlander newspaper, which he shares with his wife Tracey, and his new book on folklore and rural crafts is due to be published by The History Press in Spring 2020. When not writing, Mark also produces and narrates audiobooks both on a freelance basis and with the production company Circle of Spears, which he co-owns with Tracey and a third partner.

Links:

Website: www.thefolklorepodcast.com

Facebook: www.facebook.com/marknormanfolklore and

www.facebook.com/thefolklorepodcast

Twitter: @folklorepod and @Mr_Mark_Norman

Tracey Norman

Tracey Norman writes in several genres, including children's, fantasy, horror and non-fiction. She is currently enjoying success with her first stage play WITCH, a historical drama based on original English witch trial transcripts, which premiered in 2016 and recently enjoyed its 75th performance, which was also its London premiere. It has been used as Theatre In Education for Years 8 and 9 and for Exeter and Bristol University undergrads. She also writes a regular folklore column for the Dartmoor newspaper The Moorlander and is the researcher for The Folklore Podcast, run by her husband Mark. When she is not writing, Tracey can be found behind a microphone, as one of the voices behind Devon-based indie audio production house and theatre company Circle of Spears Productions. She is a freelance narrator on Audible and has a sizeable list of stage, TV and film credits. She gives talks to a variety of groups on historical subjects such as witchcraft and early modern medicine. She doesn't relax often, but when she does, it generally involves reading, coffee and her slightly unhealthy obsession with sock yarn. She lives near the edge of a forest in mid Devon with her husband Mark, her daughter, an insane hamster and a feline trip hazard.

Links

www.traceynormanswitch.com
www.thefireeyeschronicles.co.uk
www.circleofspears.com
Facebook@TraceyNormansWITCHBook @CircleofSpears
@TraceyNormanAuthor
Twitter @WITCHplayCoS @fireeyeschron @CircleofSpears
Instagram @Aamena2019

P.J. Reed

P.J. Reed is a writer and poet from England. She holds a BAEd from Canterbury Christ Church University, an MA from Bradford University and has dabbled in psychology with the OU. She lives in Devon with two daughters, one rescue hound, and a feral cat called Sammy. She is an outrageously eclectic writer.

Her work has appeared in a wide variety of online and print magazines, anthologies, and collections.

She is the author of the eBook 'Bad Decisions' series - a collection of macabre tales set in Ashdurton a sinister small town, set in the heart of Devon, England.

'Cutty Dyer' is the fourth short story in the 'Bad Decisions' eBook series available to download from Amazon.

P.J. Reed also writes the Richard Radcliffe supernatural murder mysteries.

She is on Twitter at https://twitter.com/PJReed_author

For more information about her writing visit website https://pjreedwriting.wixsite.com/horror

Chip Tolson

I grew up in the West Country. After national service I worked in the ship-owning industry in Liverpool, Plymouth, London, the Far East and Edinburgh. My wife and I live on Exmoor.

Since studying creative writing as a mature student at Middlesex University I have independently published a collection of twenty-three short stories titled *PEBBLES*, some of which have won competition prizes; and two novels; the first, *REQUIEM FOR PRIVATE HUGHES*, is set in the 1950s Malayan Emergency and in West Somerset, also *BIRCHLAND HALL*, set in West Yorkshire.

I've written short plays, some performed in London, Yorkshire and Brooklyn, New York, also short film scripts. My film script *Sandscape* was filmed by Somerset Film in 2017.

My website can be found at: www.chiptolson.com

Brian Willis

I'm Brian Willis, seventy three years old, retired Cambridge University Technician.

I moved with my wife Barbara to Tiverton Devon from Suffolk some sixteen years ago.

I am a short story writer and poet and a member of THE EXETER AUTHORS ASSOCIATION.

My first short story : War Story :-was inspired by visiting a church yard with a memorial to the German first World War dead while on holiday in Austria in the Nineteen Seventies.

The second : The Twyford Curse :- whilst I was driving through a Mid-Devon village on a winter Sunday evening and not seeing any sign of life.

We hope that you have enjoyed reading these stories

As independently published authors, we have no huge marketing machine, no bottomless budget. We rely on our readers to help us gain attention for our work. And next to the readers; reviews, either by word of mouth or online remain one of our most important assets.

Talking about this book, telling your friends and family and reviews on websites helps bring it to the attention of other readers. If you've enjoyed reading this book, please would you consider leaving a review, even if it's only a few words, it will be appreciated and might just help someone else discover their next great read!

Thank you.

Printed in Poland
by Amazon Fulfillment
Poland Sp. z o.o., Wrocław

56528863R00136